The Forgotten Child

By

Lorhainne Eckhart

This is a work of fiction. Names, characters, places, and incidents are either the product of the author's imagination or are used fictitiously, and any resemblance to actual persons living or dead, business establishments, events, or locales, is entirely coincidental.

The Forgotten Child

Contact Information: Lorhainne@LorhainneEckhart.com

Cover Art by Delilah K. Stephans

Editor: WildAboutBones

ISBN-13: 978-0987822635
ISBN-10: 0987822632

Discover other Titles by Lorhainne Eckhart

The Forgotten Child
The Captain's Lady

Walk the Right Road Series
The Choice

Young Adult Fiction
A Father's Love

www.LorhainneEckhart.com

To My Children

Chapter One

Every woman, at one time in her life, will experience the phrase, *I had an epiphany*. Well that's exactly what happened this particular spring morning when Emily Nelson's eyes popped open just as the sliver of light at the break of dawn crept up the horizon and, for a moment, there was peace. Until she blinked a couple of times and reality set in. She glimpsed the lump beside her in their king-size bed—her husband, Bob. Emily pushed back her thick, dark hair and slid to the side of the bed. She was hit by irritating turmoil, an unwelcome friend, twisting up her insides as if wringing out a wet rag. Not even a shred of interest existed for the man she once loved. She'd more empathy for the crotchety old geezer at the end of the street.

So what made this morning different? She didn't know how to explain this awakening unfolding from deep inside, some place she thought had long since closed and sealed off. Find some courage. Believe enough in herself and then she'd soon be living a life that was hers, for the first time, filled with an amazing peace and hope. And that's what compelled Emily to shake off her ten-year funk, throw her thin, pale legs over the side of the bed and get up.

Emily, a thirty-five-year-old average looking mother and wife, slipped on the ugly brown bathrobe her husband bought her this past Christmas. The one he meant to give his mother but got confused after he wrapped them since the boxes were identical. His mother got the old lady polyester pants with the elastic waistband meant for Emily, so she supposed she got the better of the deal.

She held her breath when she chanced a glance at Bob

who lay softly snoring on his side of the big bed; the fact he was still asleep eased her anxiety. She suppressed a sigh of relief. She had no interest in spending time in a room with this man, any more than the grumpy old geezer up the street. Maybe that was why the knot in her tummy loosened when she left the room and stood outside daughter's door. Katy, her blonde two-year-old beauty, was sleeping like an angel in the bedroom across the hall in their average, and very plain, box-style rented bungalow. Emily tiptoed across the cheap neutral colored carpeting, the same quality you see in most rental homes which showed every stain imaginable, even after shampooing year after year. She pressed her hand on the doorframe and pulled Katy's door closed so she wouldn't hear Emily at this early hour. Five a.m. was her time, when her head was clear, when her creative juices flowed, when she faced reality and could make the tough decisions with absolute clarity.

Today's the day, when he comes down, I'll say it. Her gut twisted, and she knew now it was nothing more than fear of the unknown. She couldn't wait anymore; it had to be today. It was past time and she knew she'd ignored this decision for too long. The signs were all around her—they had been for months. Now, with no chance to think it to death or get cold feet, the floor squeaked as his heavy footsteps traipsed down the hall toward her. Her skin chilled and she had a buzzing sensation in her ears, as if the floor was about to drop out from beneath her feet. Bob, her husband of twelve years, shuffled into the kitchen past her as she leaned against the counter. What made it worse was the way he looked away, as if to dismiss her, a woman of no importance.

"It's over between us." *Wow, she said it.* Her courage wavered but she crossed her arms over her small breasts and stood her ground, feeling enormous in the bulky robe even though she kept her body slim with womanly curves.

Bob turned and, for the first time in months, he really

looked at her. His dirty blonde hair was gelled and impeccably groomed. His pale face flushed and his icy blue eyes appeared so dull and tiny in his round face. His body was ordinary, average height and build—a man who wouldn't stand out in a crowd. She felt nothing for him, just a hardness; whatever love had been was now long dead and gone.

Time stretched out painfully; it took an eternity to pump the blood through her body, roaring louder and louder in her ears between breaths. He turned away. He poured himself a cup of the coffee she'd freshly brewed, dismissing her again. He'd mastered that skill long ago, hammering her pride down a little further each and every day. No wonder it took an act of sheer courage for Emily to look strangers in the eye. Hadn't her dad done it to her own mom?

"You know we haven't had a marriage for a long time. There are no feelings left between us. We don't communicate and Katy's picking up on the tension in this house."

He dropped his mug on the counter and fired off his own delusion. "I don't know what you're talking about. I think you're the one with the problem. Katy's fine if you're not around." His words stung, even though she knew it wasn't true. Why didn't she expect this? Because her mind didn't play those kinds of games, that's why.

"No Katy is *not* fine. You're always yelling at her. You won't spend time with her. When you're home, you sit in front of the TV twenty-four/seven. You do nothing to help me."

Shouting, he stepped toward her, "You know what I think this is really about? Money! Anyway, it's your fault we have no money!"

Okay here we go. She expected an attack. He was really good at twisting things to his way of thinking. This man she married, at one time loved, had become an unwelcome stranger. "I think it has to do with no communication. The only time I know what's new with you is when I overhear you on the phone. You know … those nightly conversations with your mother. And come to think of it, that's part of the problem. The only relationship you have is with your mother. And it's just plain weird. You're not a child. Grow up. It's disturbing that you talk to her about what's going on in your life and not me. If you were being honest with yourself, you'd admit you've made no attempt to have a relationship with me. And I've ignored how you've treated me for years."

Emily held up the flat of her trembling hand, unable to stop her mouth from spewing everything she'd suppressed for so long. She continued, "You've always had this strange relationship with your Mom. What's really sick is I've had to stoop to eavesdropping when you're on the phone with her. Just to find out your latest news. A vacation you're planning with friends of yours. A new job you're applying for in Seattle; taking a few courses at night school. Don't you think as your wife I have a right to know about these things?"

He dumped his coffee down the sink. His face hardened into someone she didn't know. "It wasn't as if I was hiding it from you, but you're sure happy to launch a war with my family. You could've have just asked."

Emily shut her eyes and let out a heavy sigh. Katy would be awake soon and Bob needed to leave for work. "This is going nowhere. I'm not going to keep fighting with you. I'd like you to move out. Take whatever you want."

He didn't answer her. What he did was grab his coat and storm out the door, slamming it behind him hard enough to rattle the double pane windows. But apparently, he wasn't done with his temper tantrum because he followed up with gunning the engine of two-door rusted Cavalier, the tires squealing down the driveway. Katy screamed. Across the street, lights came on in the front window of the Hanson's, house. Great. She'd need to apologize for Bob disturbing them before six a.m. with his irresponsible behavior.

Emily raced down the hall to comfort her daughter, furious at Bob for yet another mess he'd created for her to clean up. Except this time, it didn't stick—the mad, that is. She felt the dark, oppressive weight lifting from her back, leaving her with a light peaceful feeling flowing through her body. You know, the one you get when you know you've finally done the right thing. Even though she had no money, no job, a child and no idea how she'd make ends meet. A dismal sounding outcome but, for the first time in years, she felt the sun shoot out a powerful ray of hope.

Chapter Two

The morning hadn't gone as planned. Emily's faced glowed as she reached down to pick up the morning paper. It hadn't quite made it to the curb forcing her to step out into the street close to where the Hansons were out digging up their yard. She'd apologized yesterday, and even though they'd been gracious in their response, Emily still felt responsible for Bob's childish behavior. And it was Mr. Hanson, not Mrs. Hanson who questioned Emily on what had upset Bob. This left Emily cornered; so she'd confessed she'd asked Bob to leave. This left them frowning, and speechless, which wasn't a good thing.

"Hello," was all she could say this morning before darting back into the house. She didn't make eye contact because she didn't want to explain more. Mr. Hanson could talk her ear off, and by now, he'd most likely have a few words of advice to share with her.

Emily leaned against the closed door. Worry and, in her chest, a nightmarish pressure began building and pressing, stronger and harder, until the simple art of breathing became a gigantic struggle. It was her head, her mind, creating the problems. She'd fall flat on her face. She couldn't make it alone. How would she look after Katy? What if she couldn't get a job? Instead of focusing on the present, her thoughts jumped from the past to the future with what ifs, could haves and should haves. "Stop it!" She kicked a pink, fluffy stuffed animal across the room and stubbed her little toe on the corner of the table. "Ah crap." She hopped on one foot exhaling sharply. After a minute she hobbled to the kitchen counter.

She should have started looking for a job yesterday

after she'd asked Bob to leave. But she didn't because of a whole pile of excuses. Katy had been cranky all day after waking up so early after Bob's tantrum. Then she had to feed, bathe and put Katy to bed, all before Bob, still moody, dragged his sorry ass through the door, telling her he'd found a furnished apartment in Olympia during his lunch hour. He'd move out on the weekend. She almost shouted, "Hallelujah!"

But now this morning, she felt the after effects of an adrenaline rush, maybe that's why she was in such a crappy mood. She muttered a curse as she opened the damp newspaper to the classified section. It was sparse today, the feed store, the market. The one that stood out was the one in bold at the bottom of the page:

Wanted: Caregiver and Cook

Duties include day-to-day care of a young child.

"I can do that." She slapped the paper and glanced up at Katy who was watching *Dora* on TV as she snuggled with her blanket on the sofa. Emily reached behind her and snatched up the cordless telephone. She paused, pressing the top of the telephone to her forehead when a sinking fear she'd fail tried to weave its way into her, zapping away all her newfound courage. "Knock it off, just call." Emily ran her finger over the ad and dialed the number. Her heart pounded so hard it hurt her chest. Her hand shook as her adrenaline soared through her veins. To release the rapidly building tension and calm her nerves, she paced through the kitchen and living room.

"Hello." An older woman's voice chimed on the other end.

"Hi I'm calling about the ad in the paper for a caregiver and cook."

"Oh yes, that would be Brad you'd want to talk to. Just hang on a second and let me get him." Unfortunately the wait for Brad to come on the line allowed the irritable voice in Emily's head to creep in and fill her with doubts. *What do you think you're doing? You're not qualified.* Sweating, she was tempted to hang up when she heard the man's deep baritone voice.

"Hello."

Along with being tongue tied, Emily's dry throat threatened to close up. She swallowed the hard lump and licked her lips. "Hi, my name's Emily Nelson, I'm calling about your ad in the paper as a caregiver and cook for a child." She winced when her voice squeaked.

"It's for my son Trevor, he's three. I run a ranch and need someone to look after him and also do the cooking."

"Are you still interviewing for the position?"

"I am but I need someone right away. I have a ranch to run. If you're interested, could you come out to the Ranch?"

He was abrupt. Straight to the point and that made it easier for Emily.

"I'm interested, but I should tell you I have a two year old who'll be with me at work. He said nothing. In that nanosecond, Emily felt the impending rejection. And that awful voice chimed in, *No, I don't think it'll work. I need someone without kids.*

"Could you be here at nine tomorrow morning?" This she didn't expect.

"Nine, no problem I'll be there." She committed to a time she knew darn well wouldn't work. Katy had a checkup scheduled with her pediatrician tomorrow at nine. How was she going to do both? How stupid and desperate was that? *Say something.* But she didn't. She swallowed and continued scribbling down the address, along with rough directions to the ranch, on the back of her overdue hydro bill. It was not far from town, maybe a twenty-minute drive.

Emily held the disconnected phone, and then tapped her head with it again. "Stupid, you forgot to ask what he's paying, the hours, come on, Emily." She dropped the phone back in its charger, realizing he too hadn't asked many questions. What about her qualifications, experience and references?

Emily dug out a pen and paper and started a list. She needed to be prepared for tomorrow, so she scribbled down a list of questions. Most importantly, she needed to someone to take Katy to the doctor.

* * * *

Early the next morning, she opened the front door to her bubbly friend Gina, a vivacious, trim woman with short dark hair. Under her wool cape, she wore a turtleneck and blue jeans. She burst through the door and hugged Emily hard. "Morning, darling. I hope you have some coffee. I only had time for a quick cup before bolting over here."

"What about Fred and your boys? Aren't they going to miss you this morning?"

She waved her hand as she wiped her shoes and wandered into the small box style kitchen. "You should have seen the lost look on their faces this morning. It was priceless, my husband and two teenage boys, horrified that I actually expected them to fend for themselves this morning. Hey there cutie pie."

Katy practically leapt into Gina's arms. Gina knew how to get down on the floor and play hard with kids on their level. "Thank you, Gina, for coming. I'm nervous enough as it is about this interview without dragging a two year old with me and I forgot about her appointment with the pediatrician. It took me months to get it and I didn't want to reschedule with this guy..." She was rambling and she knew it, so she shut her mouth.

"Don't be nervous, you'll do just fine. And you need to give yourself some credit. You've a lot of courage. I've watched you from the sidelines these past few years as you've spiraled into a downward slide. I'm amazed, and a little awed, by what you've done. It's as if you've taken a leap off the dock without a life jacket. You have this pure faith now—everything will work out. Now hold onto that and move forward. Don't look back." Gina glanced down at her small gold Rolex, a gift from her husband for their anniversary last month. You better go. You have enough time to get your head together and enjoy the drive. Remember don't rush … that's when you get flustered."

Emily hugged and kissed both her daughter and friend, pulled on her brown wool coat and grabbed her purse and handwritten resume. Gina was right; having extra time to find where she needed to go relieved a lot of her anxiety, as did being alone. She took a deep breath and pulled out of her driveway.

Thick trees lined both sides of the road out of town. This was a peaceful drive. She realized she'd never driven west of town in the ten years she'd lived in Hoquiam. She'd grown up in Seattle and that was where she'd met Bob. Hoquiam seemed like a nice place to live after he was offered a government job in Olympia ten years earlier. The commute was not too long, and Emily's dream of living in a small community had never left her. Now as she drove these narrow winding roads, passing only a few cars through this private, rural and heavily forested part of the peninsula, she was reminded of her childhood dream.

Emily balanced the hastily scribbled directions on the steering wheel. She passed the faded red barn at the second marker on the highway. Making a right turn onto a gravel road, she continued down until she saw the split rail fencing with 665 in bright green numbers embedded in the wood. A huge fir archway on two solid beams surrounded the entrance to the dirt driveway, with the name Echo Springs carved into the weathered wood. What was it about the name that stirred some nostalgic memory of longing in her tummy? History, established families, of Mom, Dad, grandparents passing down their heritage and land. She'd heard the powerful family names whispered in the community: the Rickson's, Folley's, *who were the others*? She was caught now by a nervous flutter continuing to pound her solar plexus as she drove down the long dirt driveway.

Old growth spruce, cedar and fir trees on both sides created a dense canopy overhead and a mixture of other bushes and trees gave the appearance of walls. At the end, it opened up into a large clearing exposing a two-story white frame house with a wraparound veranda and large post beams. It resembled an old rambling Victorian. She parked in front of the house beside an old Ford Escort, a dirty blue pick-up truck that had seen better days, a chipped yellow digger, a fairly new black GMC one ton pickup and a flatbed trailer loaded with some mysterious goods covered with a tarp. *How many people live here?*

The wind created a chilly breeze as thick clouds cluttered the baby blue sky. Emily was far from cold when she climbed out of her van. Her underarms were damp and she prayed her deodorant was strong enough to keep her from smelling ripe. *It's nerves, that's all.* Or maybe it was the five cups of high-octane coffee she'd guzzled before Gina arrived, which wound her nerves so tight she could have bounced her way to the door.

She paused and breathed deep the clean air. The front of the house was virtually bare of any landscaping. Patches of grass poked up here and there from the well-packed dirt in the front yard. The flowerbeds in front were littered with dead perennials, weeds and overgrown grass long and bare leaning against the house. *How many acres did he have?* A large barn and other outbuildings littered the property with what looked like miles of open land with a spectacular view of the mountains.

She flexed her damp hands and climbed the four white wooden steps. She noticed the paint was chipped. Emily nearly tripped when the third step suddenly creaked and caught her off guard. She was way out of her comfort zone and this didn't help, prompting her self-doubt to send SOS signals to confuse her already shaky insides. She was a mess. Her face ached so much, she was positive the forced smile she wore looked more like a grimace. Emily clutched a brown manila envelope stuffed with her resume and references from her friends. On unsteady legs, she crossed the wide porch. A porch made for families to gather at the end of the day to laugh together and share dreams and triumphs. Something families did. Well back to reality, it was a dream family Emily yearned to be part of. She spied a wooden swing suspended by chains at the far end of the porch beside two wicker chairs placed on each side of a large picture window and she sighed.

She could daydream about this imaginary family abode all day but when she faced the classic wooden frame door, Emily's dry throat threatened to close up. "Well it's now or never." So she did it. She rapped on the door with a couple of confident solid knocks. Her heart pounded, echoing with a thud in her ears when she heard solid, heavy footsteps approach. She swallowed and felt a notorious bright scarlet flush flame her face.

She wanted to hide in that anxiety panicked second but it was too late when the door flew open. She stepped back clutching her purse to her chest like a shield and fidgeted with her old wool coat, pulling it tight around her. A tall, broad shouldered man filled the doorway. She was struck speechless by this man with hazy brown eyes. He didn't have pretty boy features. What he had was a solid, strong jaw, a hardness to his square face and eyes alive with some ancient wisdom, making him the most handsome man she'd ever seen. His flannel plaid shirt didn't cover any average man. This was a well-formed man who she'd swear could make a burlap sack look good. He pulled off a pair of reading glasses and gazed at her, looking confused, as if she were a door-to-door sales girl, obviously wondering why she was on his doorstep. She hated that feeling.

"Hi, I'm…" Then the worst thing that could possibly happen, happened. She fumbled her purse upside down. It tipped open scattering the contents of her bag as well as coins from the unzipped coin purse inside all over the doorway floor, along with what remained of her dignity.

Chapter Three

Mortified, the ringing in her ears catapulted her tingling body to what she could only explain as an out of body experience. Who was this idiot who'd taken over her body? Her face burned crimson, again. And she did what any self-respecting woman would do. She dropped to her knees, grabbed the coins, open wallet, crackers, Katy's toys and the wrapped sanitary napkin lying by his feet. Emily stuffed everything back in her purse, cursing her idiocy at not making sure it was zipped up. Wasn't that rule number one?

Retreating into her head, she prayed, maybe at some point in the years to come, she'd look back on this and laugh. Except now to make things worse, Mr. Good-looking knelt down in front of her, nose to nose and started scooping up her loose coins scattered across the hardwood floor. Emily glanced up; his eyes were burning into her and she wanted nothing more than to slink away apologizing profusely, run to her van and drive away so she could cry the tears threatening to burn a hole in her head. "I'm so sorry; I can't believe I did this." Why did he have to help? Why couldn't he ignore what she'd done? He said nothing as he handed her the loose coins. She dumped everything into her plain black purse and zipped it up. Emily then sprung to her feet without looking, smacking her head into his, which sent her tumbling back down where she landed on her derriere.

"Wait. Don't move. Let me help you up. Are you okay?"

Could it get any worse? She wanted to weep right here, right now, but she was stronger than that, right? She rubbed her head and the strong man held out his large, rough hand and with little effort, pulled her up. Back where she started from, facing this extraordinary tall man, who shoved his hands in his front pockets as he appeared to study her with amazing control, no sign of embarrassment, but an odd curiosity twinkled in those wise whiskey colored eyes.

Without a doubt, he must think she was nuts, a moron. Maybe he'd ask her to leave. Her forced smile pulled at her mouth.

"I'm Emily Nelson. I called about the job in the paper, we spoke…" The telephone rang. He turned and walked away.

He abandoned her inside the doorway as if she was a woman of no importance and hurried in the direction of the ringing phone. Unsure of what to do, Emily shuffled from one foot to the other, this time looping her cursed bulky purse over her shoulder. He shouted from around the corner, "Come in, have a seat. Sorry, I need to take this."

Emily wiped her boots on the mat before stepping onto the light hardwood floor and closed the door behind her. The wide entryway was filled with a large gold plated encrusted mirror, something a woman who liked the finer things would have insisted upon. She caught her perky image in the entryway mirror along with white spots, which were most likely Katy's milk, on the lapel of her tired old coat. Her plain mousy long hair was pulled back in her usual ponytail. She was by no means gorgeous but her friends labeled her cute, like a shorter, brown-haired Meg Ryan. She brushed at the milk stain again, gave up, stepped past the mirror and went around the corner, which opened into a large living room done up in earth tones with a rock face fireplace on the east wall. The furnishings were exquisite, dark brown leather, with a lot of wood, very masculine. But the hint of a feminine touch was everywhere, in the framed artwork, carvings, floral rug and designer cushions, all coordinated and tastefully arranged. Guided by the rumble of his voice, she crossed through the living room and faced a large oval archway which opened into a square country kitchen. In the middle sat a solid oak table, surrounded by ten wooden straight back chairs, enough to sit and feed a large family. And there he was, striding back and forth, with the phone pressed to his ear. He didn't glance up. Instead turned his back. His scuffed black cowboy boots squeaked on the worn wood floor. Emily gazed at her ruggedly handsome potential employer who arrogantly oozed deep alpha male, a man with priorities, self-confidence and rude. *Give him a break, maybe he's just busy.*

He hung up the phone and let out a hard sigh before turning to face Emily. He had his hands on his hips, and then gestured one toward her as he stalked in the room. "Let's sit in the living room here."

Emily darted a glance at the clutter free, extremely neat living room behind her. The plump, green cushions on each end of the high amber sofa, added to the warm pleasant vibes bouncing off the art laden walls. All the oil paintings had a western motif: lone cowboys, horses and western murals. Beside the sofa, but under the large picture window, was a solid oak toy box filled with toys neatly put away.

As Emily walked past the large flat screen TV on her way to the three-seat sofa, she noted the clutter free end tables; nothing valuable was within a child's reach. A homemade brown and orange afghan was carelessly tossed over the back of the couch. It was pure instinct for Emily to fold it and lay it over the back of the couch. She turned and allowed the back of her legs to touch the sofa, but she didn't sit.

"Please sit down Emily." He extended out the flat of his hand, very much in control.

"Ah, thank you." She perched on the edge of the soft leather seat across from a man who was too damn good to look at—a man obviously comfortable in his own skin.

Hardness set his jaw as he studied her. The tick of the wall clock seemed to echo in the silence and Emily squirmed in her seat. *Why was he looking at her like that?* Maybe it was her outrageous entrance and he was wondering what kind of kook she was, whether he could entrust her with his child. Yes, that had to be it.

She swallowed hard. "I'm Emily Nelson; I talked to you yesterday on the phone about the job."

He blinked before closing those exquisite eyes as if he'd forgotten the reason she was here. When he opened them again, his hard judgmental expression seemed to have softened a bit.

He extended his large hand, taking hers in a firm grip. Just the touch of his solid calloused hand and the secure squeeze was enough to teeter her nerves back to that awkward woman at the door. She wondered what it would be like to have a man like this run his hands over you. She snatched her hand back before her face burned any brighter. "The name's Brad Friessen." Emily kept quiet. He didn't run on with his words. He must be a deep thinker, a doer. She could relate to that but not him. Her sly eyes glanced down at his left hand, no gold band, no white line, no wife or significant other. Or maybe he was one of those arrogant guys who wouldn't wear a ring, a lady's man. He had the looks and the attitude. Now was the time to ask about the woman who answered the phone when she called. Who was she?

"This is a working ranch I run and I need a woman to look after my son. I'm old fashioned in my values. Children should be at home, not stuck in daycare. I'm looking for someone who's comfortable in a kitchen and looking after children: a role that should come natural to a woman. I don't want someone who's got the phone stuck to their ear half the day. It's a decent job and good pay, $500 a week, room and board and includes all your meals."

Her heart sank about the same time the bottom

dropped out of her stomach. It was too good to be true. She wanted to cry. "I have a little girl, I didn't realize..."

His face hardened and he looked away. He was angry with her … no, furious. She didn't know what to say when he let out a heavy sigh. He closed his eyes, rubbing his hand over the light brown shadow that appeared over his jaw. He faced her again with those deep brown eyes now turned to steel. He could be a hard man.

"What, not enough money for you? I can't stand the games you women play." He lowered his voice. But it didn't take the bite from his words. Holy crap what kind of trip was this guy on? Was it just her he had a problem with or all women? "Mr. Friessen…"

"Brad," he cut her off his palm held up flat, a man used to having his way.

"Sorry … Brad. It's not about money. Your offer is quite generous. I have a little girl and, the thing is, I guess I just assumed I would come here to work during the day and then go home. I rent a place in town. I'm recently separated, *almost*, and Katy lives with me. She's two, so I'd be bringing her with me during the day to work and…" She was babbling and knew it when he cut her off.

"I need someone to be here all day. And there's the matter of the cooking. It's all three meals and breakfast's early."

"Brad, I'm a little confused, are you still offering me a job knowing I've a child who'll be here with me?

He leaned back looking much more relaxed than he had earlier, a man back in control, his hand tapped the back of the sofa.

"There's room in this house, lots of unused bedrooms upstairs. This is a big job. You'd be required to look after my son and do all the cooking. I have two hired hands who eat here, well, sometimes. They live in a small house I have on the property behind the barn. I have a woman who comes in twice a week to clean, so you'd only need to keep up the house in between. Still interested?"

Emily slid forward and raised her palms, only to press them onto her knees. "Yes, I'm interested. Are you offering me the job, I mean you haven't even asked about my experience, references or if I've had a criminal record check." Emily fumbled for the envelope and pulled out the sheet of hand written references.

"I'd need you to start right away." He uncrossed his legs and reached for the paper, dropping his gaze to scan her list of names. He peered up at her seconds later.

"Can you cook?"

"Yes."

"Are you a criminal?"

"No, unless you count a speeding ticket I got two years ago."

"Only one?" The tension that drove this meeting a few moments ago changed. The lighthearted teasing burst the bubble of worry building inside her tummy. She breathed easier, anticipating that maybe there was something really good just around the corner.

"I'd need to be assured my son would take priority. If you're bringing your daughter, will you be able to do the cooking and still look after him, and not ignore him?"

"I wouldn't neglect your son but I won't neglect my daughter either. I can look after both easily. I'm a mother. It's what I do." Emily swirled her hand in the air.

He was quiet again. For the life of her, she couldn't read his expression. What was he thinking?

"Could you start tomorrow?"

Her ears were ringing. And she wondered if she'd heard him right. "Well yes, that'd be fine. But I can't move us that quickly. I have a whole house to pack up."

"How about coming for the day until we can work out the rest of the details, at least then you can get comfortable with Trevor, and he you, until you move here."

"All right, tomorrow I'll come with Katy. Is about eight-thirty okay?"

"Sounds good."

This was too easy. Brad slapped his hands on his knees, stood and, magically, he appeared taller, like an enormous weight had been lifted off his shoulders. He hovered over her. Emily glanced at her purse and gave an extra tug on the zipper to make sure it was closed before slipping it over her shoulder. She held tight as she stood before this sizeable man.

"I have a good feeling about this Emily. There's something about you. I think this arrangement will work for both of us. I love my boy and only want the best for him."

He escorted her to the door. "Tomorrow then, Brad. And thank you for the job."

She bumped his hand when she awkwardly turned to shake it. Lord, she truly was a klutz today. She cursed her lack of self-esteem which, at times, kept her from being fit for polite society. And making it worse, he grabbed her by the shoulders, before she could knock something over, and guided her through the door. Her face heated again, bright red. She tried to duck her head but as she stood outside the door, she was forced to face him when he held open the white screen door—a replica she was sure was from the 1930's.

He looked over her head, obviously sensing her discomfort, and shoved his hand in his pocket and leaned his other arm on top of the screen door. His sleeves were rolled up to his elbows showing off his tanned, well-sculpted forearms. Before she could turn away, he pulled his hand from his pocket and extended it.

She placed her hand in his; he squeezed, not too tight, but a nice, friendly handshake to seal the deal. "Drive safely Emily. Let me know when you can make arrangements on your end to move, I'll send my men to help."

"Wow, thank you." She was sweating again, and then remembered the woman who'd answered the phone when she'd called. Better to ask now so she didn't worry and wonder all night because she didn't ask. "What about

Trevor's mother, was that who answered the phone?" A dark shadow cast over and hardened his good-looking face to one harboring something dark filled with nothing pleasant. *There's a problem.* His cheek twitched.

"No. That was Mary Haske, my neighbor who helps me out." A sharp bite filled his tone, nothing nice and friendly now. "You'll meet her. She's an old family friend I've known since I was a kid. Trevor's mother doesn't live here or see Trevor."

The way the man held back his fury, she sensed she'd just peeled away a well crusted over scab, put there by a woman who'd broken his heart and done something this man hated her for. *Don't piss him off.* Yah, she heard the warning. She knew some people didn't forgive; they held onto the hate, letting it become a monkey on their back.

She swallowed hard, and then backed away. "I'll see you tomorrow."

Chapter Four

Her hands wrapped around the steering wheel, driving alone became a mini-holiday, one she rarely enjoyed. It gave her time to think, evaluate her life, dream big and put plans in place. That's just what she did now after the unusual interview. "I'll give notice to the landlord, pack after Katy's in bed, could maybe be ready by the weekend. Yah, this will be easy." In some ways, this change would be a relief.

Gina must have been glued to the window when Emily pulled into the driveway. Before Emily could turn off the ignition, she'd ripped open the door and bounced outside with Katy perched on her hip.

Her little blonde princess clapped and squealed with glee, holding her arms out for her mama. The rusted hinges on the van door squeaked when Emily gave it a shove, just as Katy landed in her arms. Emily inhaled her baby soft scent and held her tight, kissing her over and over on her plump round cheeks. "I've got the job, baby girl and we start tomorrow."

"Yeah! Oh, I knew you could do it." Gina punched her lean arms in the air before pulling her and Katy into a hug. "It's freezing out here, come on. So tell me everything, details, details. Who you're working for?" Gina clapped her hands to hurry Emily inside.

Emily left her coat and shoes on as she carried Katy into the darkened living room, where her worn out brilliant green couch had seen better days. She dropped into her Scottish plaid glider rocker and let out a sigh, a contented sound, like every burden inside was gone. She put Katy down on the ugly beige carpet where she toddled off to pick up her dolly with bluc ink stains streaked across its plastic face. Emily watched as she plopped the doll into the doll-sized stroller parked by the fireplace and began to push her around the living room. "We need to move to his ranch."

"Move, why?" Gina perched across from Emily on the edge of the dark green sofa.

"The job's full time care of his young son. He's a single father and runs the ranch alone. He needs someone there to cook breakfast, lunch and dinner. It's what I do now, except now I'll be getting paid for it."

"Does he have a house on his property for you to live in?" Gina flattened both her hands across her knees.

"We'll be moving into his house. It's large and there's enough room." There was a slight hitch in Emily's voice. And Gina being Gina, never missed anything and could make anyone trying to keep the slightest detail from her squirm, narrowed her dark brown eyes and stiffened her spine as she leaned forward.

"Call it a gift from my mother side, but honey I'm one Irish Italian girl you can't pull nothing over on, and there's a whole schwack of problems with that arrangement and I know you're holding something back from me. So you may as well spill it, all of it."

Emily looked up at the low dingy stucco ceiling and rocked the squeaky chair. She answered without meeting the narrowed eyes that burned another layer off Emily's protective shell. "He's the most attractive man I've ever met, and arrogant and unforgiving, and I humiliated myself like the bumbling, socially inept idiot that I am. And Trevor, that's his little boy, the mother's not around. I don't know what happened to her, but it's evidently a sore point with him. One he's not willing to discuss, and he doesn't hold her too highly in his regard, which I suspect is where he puts all women."

"Oh, I see." Gina rose to her feet when the kettle whistled from the kitchen. She walked around the bargain basement square coffee table and paused. "Emily darling, you best make sure you go into this with both eyes open. I see that dreamy look you're trying your damnedest to hide from me. Don't forget, you've just kicked out a no good for nothing dog. You're vulnerable, guys, predators who're up to no good read that, and will take advantage. Make sure this stays business. Because right now you're on the rebound and I know you're dreaming about meeting a real man, except you need time to heal first. So you best hide that googly-eyed drool and forget you think he's the finest looking man you've ever seen, so he doesn't go and take advantage of you."

Emily felt the downy hair on the back of her neck rise like thorny barbed wire. How could Gina say something like that to her? So what if it was true? She couldn't shake the irritation caused by Gina's blunt implication that she was so much of a ditz that she'd check her brains and fall at this guy's feet. She had good sense and sound judgment. How dare she?

"Oh knock off the wounded pride thing." She hadn't moved. The kettle still shrilled in the kitchen. So Emily gripped the arm of the rocker and started to get up.

"Sit down, Em. As your friend, I have the right to point out some potentially dangerous pitfalls. Friends watch each other's back, especially when we've checked our heads in the nearest closet. This hot to trot arrogant guy's your boss. You make sure you protect yourself. He sounds volatile and men like that can be real jerks. You're living in his house. Different rules apply, a mutual respect for one. Katy will be there; make sure it stays comfortable for her."

Gina leaned down and kissed Emily on the forehead, and then raced into the kitchen to silence the piercing kettle. Emily closed her eyes and rocked. When Emily opened her eyes, her bright blue-eyed angel watched her as if she understood every word and knew what sudden change was about to happen.

Emily reached out her overworked hand with short, square nails and torn cuticles—a hand she knew would never be featured on any ivory dish soap commercial. They were dry, plain and serviceable. But her darling Katy didn't care. They were filled with love and that's all Katy wanted as she gripped Emily's fingers and climbed on her mother's lap.

Gina called out from the kitchen. "So how soon do we move you?"

Emily couldn't keep the lightness from invading her voice. She smiled lovingly down on her daughter who rested her pinkish cheek against Emily's full breast, her eyelids lowered, becoming too much of an effort to keep open, while she sucked her soother. "As soon as I can pack. Brad would like us there like yesterday."

Gina reappeared through the archway dividing the kitchen from the small living and dining room. She leaned against the cheap looking white wall beside the fireplace as she frowned. She crossed her arms as a sharp twinkling of light sparked in her eyes, and then rubbed her chin with her index finger and thumb, back and forth, a telltale sign Gina was formulating plans.

"I'm taking Katy to work with me tomorrow."

"Okay, I'll make some calls, get people here to help pack. But that's after you go to work tomorrow and, if all's well and this turns out to be the blessing you so deserve, you can give notice to your landlord tomorrow night. Not before."

She was good and Emily knew if there ever was a crisis, Gina was the one you wanted in your corner to handle things. A former secretary, producer and the driving force behind her husband's successful glass shop. You were wise to hand her the keys and let her handle things. These mundane details could overwhelm Emily, where Gina could step in, dissect and arrange a sound viable plan, with color-coded categories highlighted on the notes she was sure to produce. Yah, she could hardly wait.

****

The next morning before Bob left, Emily dropped the little bomb that she'd obtained a job and would be moving. His glowing response, which was not unexpected, with flushed cheeks burning crimson, was his mouth falling open from obvious shock. Oops, guess she read that right. He'd expected her to land flat on her face, but to hell with him and his expectation for her to come crawling back. Hell would freeze over before she'd ever consider it. No, she was almost free. And to prove it, Gina arrived right before Emily left for her first day of work at the ranch with three pages color coded by priority. What Emily needed to do, along with numbers and contact names, which included the lawyer to handle her legal separation, the gas and electric company, notice to the post office for change of address and one page of sensible questions to ask Brad, which Emily, in her fog of excitement should have thought of, but didn't.

Wow! She scanned the checklist, hugged Gina and then hurried with Katy to the van, in awe of the organizational skills of this woman.

And even though Gina offered once again to keep Katy with her this morning, Emily knew how imperative today was. Today with Katy would be to test the waters, sink or swim, as the old saying goes, and find out just how smoothly—she hoped, no believed, it would go. "It'll work out." It had to, since she was uprooting Katy to a home that wasn't hers. Children needed stability so as Emily drove through the familiar gates of Echo Springs, past the split rail fence framing each side of the long winding, well-treed entrance, where the dirt and gravel road looked freshly grated. Emily felt a sudden spiral rise from the pit of her stomach up through her chest, as if she'd been drop-kicked into her future, without having any chance to analyze, a.k.a. question her sanity, and back out.

And it was a good thing too, since Brad was waiting outside his lovely Victorian in the bare front yard. All that pure, masculine power, six feet two inches of ruggedness. How could a man wearing a worn tan barn jacket exude all those damn fine, good-looking vibes? "Oh shit." Without Katy to keep her distracted from those magnificent see-right-into-your-soul whiskey colored eyes, she'd probably trip over both her feet.

Emily parked her van and focused on taking the keys out and zipping up her purse. When she looked up through the window, Brad lifted a little boy bundled in a dark blue hoodie up onto his shoulders. He swaggered toward Emily in a way that said he owned, and was proud of, this land. Emily opened her door and tried to contain the shake in her hand. She slammed her door and hurried around to the passenger side to slide the side door open.

"You made it." She could smell his earthy fragrance, no sandalwood, as she craned her neck up. His smile was intoxicating and today he was much more relaxed, nicer. Maybe, if he'd be a jerk again, she could relax.

"We did." Okay how stupid was that. Emily turned away before her face grew any redder and focused on unbuckling Katy from her booster, and lifted her.

"So who's this?" His voice was teasing, light and riddled with tenderness. He was a different man from yesterday and he didn't ignore Katy, just the opposite, he reached over and tickled her chin. Hooray, another completed checkmark on Gina's detailed laundry list—the list to reorganize Emily's life.

"This is my daughter Katy. Katy, this is Brad, the man I told you about." She giggled and clammed up that sweet pert little mouth, in a too-shy ploy she always launched upon meeting anyone new. Emily was positive this was just the beginning of the ploys she'd play on many a man to wrap around her finger. "Sorry, she's shy, but wait until she warms up to you, then she won't stop talking."

He laughed with such genuine warmth, for an instant

Emily wondered if he was the same difficult man she'd met yesterday. Trevor bounced on Brad's shoulders reciting a "Blib, blib..." until Brad put him down. He wandered to the wide rock path that led up to the front steps.

"Is this Trevor?"

"Yes, that's my boy." Brad shoved his hands in his pockets as he watched over his son.

"Hi Trevor, I'm Emily…" The little boy never turned toward her, he had no interest in her or Katy.

"How old is Trevor?" The hardness was back in Brad's face. He didn't look at her.

"Three." He cleared his throat roughly.

Trevor stopped in the middle of the rock path and dropped to his knees. He started digging with his tiny little fingers around a rock. "No Trevor." Brad lunged and swooped Trevor up.

"No, no, no." Trevor screamed over and over, flailing at Brad. His tiny-fisted hands smacked Brad on the nose.

"Stop it, Trevor. Emily's here, remember I told you she's going to look after you." But he didn't stop his screeching. In fact, he changed the words to a "whee, whee, whee" thing as Brad held his hand. "He must be tired, all this newness with you here is throwing him off." Brad shouted over his stiffened shoulder.

His anxiety was back, but of course, what an awkward moment. Was the kid always like this?

"Come inside Emily, I'll get Trevor some crackers, and then you can get started."

Katy remained quiet and still in Emily's arms, as they both watched Trevor at a safe distance. Emily shifted Katy in her arms and followed a tense and ill at ease Brad into the house.

What a difference the house was today. The neat and tidy living room with upscale leather furniture and hardwood flooring that would showcase in any home and garden magazine was a complete mess today. Emily stepped over plastic toys, puzzle boxes and pieces scattered from one end of the room to the far wall by the kitchen, with wool blankets and two afghans hanging over the sofa and scattered on the floor—a rough night or morning or something. The kitchen wasn't much better. Brad yanked open the lovely white cupboard door, the one with the tempered glass center, and grabbed a box of cheese crackers with a cartoon character on the bright red box. Katy tightened her hold around Emily's neck, as the kid screeched louder.

But Emily couldn't get past the dirty dishes, cereal boxes, discarded food packaging filling the sink and covering every bit of counter space. And the odor, what was that smell?

She turned in a circle and had to lift her foot off the sticky floor. Even though this kitchen had been recently remodeled with upscale appliances, cupboards and maybe a really nice teal green slate countertop, she wouldn't swear to it considering the state it was in.

His eyes were on her, watching her, as a frown deepened those tired lines around his eyes. She sensed him pull back, in the way men do when they think you're judging them, which she wasn't, or maybe he half expected her to turn and run out the door. "Well, I better get started, if anyone's planning on having lunch, it's going to take me a good hour or two with the kids to look after to clean up this mess."

Brad flushed. "Look, I'm sorry about this..." He gestured with a hand that held the boxed crackers. "If this is too much for you to do and look after both kids…" He didn't finish the sentence as gravel spewed from the sound of a heavy truck pulling in followed by a short blast of a horn. Emily faced the narrow hallway that led out the back of the kitchen to a back door. What sounded like a large man stomped up what she presumed were the back steps, the hinges squealed on the screen door right before the inside door, with the curtained tiny glass window, pushed opened. "Hey Brad, Dudley's here with the feed for the cattle, we need you out here." The other big man hovering in the doorway, must have been six feet, was wearing a plaid wool shirt with an orange baseball cap and what looked like several days since he'd last shaved.

Emily turned to look at Brad who closed his eyes and shook his head. "Shit. Sorry, Emily, you're on your own. I've got to take care of this. He held out Trevor to her as he shoved a handful of crackers in his mouth. Emily put Katy down beside her and Katy being unsure, promptly gripped her mother's black jeans just below the knee."

"Okay, I'm not really…" Brad paid no attention at all, as he hurried to pass her Trevor, along with the cracker box. He didn't spare her a passing glance.

"See you at lunch." And then he was gone out the back, past the whitewashed, dated paneling that filled the narrow hall, pulling the back door closed behind him. Emily couldn't believe it. She stood there holding a quiet child who had no interest in her. He should have been big eyed, maybe even scared of the stranger holding him. The only interest he had was the box of crackers.

"Mama." Katy tugged on her jeans then shoved her thumb in her mouth and reached her arms up. "Oh Katy bug, I can't hold you both." Emily squatted down and sat Trevor on the floor. When she tried to stand with the cracker box, Trevor screeched, "na, na, na." Holy crap was he loud.

"Here you go, no need to act like that. Use your words." Emily handed him the box of crackers. Again, he wouldn't look at her. For a minute, she worried he'd choke he was cramming them in his mouth so fast. Katy tapped her leg and pointed to the box. Of course, she wanted some. "Katy, how about a banana instead? She dropped her bag on the sticky cluttered table, and pulled out a banana leaving Katy's box of organic rice crackers out of site. She slid out a wooden chair and sat Katy down. "I should have brought your booster seat. I knew I forgot something." Emily slipped off her coat and rolled up her sleeves, scanning the rectangular, neglected kitchen filled with unfinished food, a sink overflowing with cups, dishes and slimy, dirty dishwater. The large white propane stove was grease covered and littered with dirty pots. She shot a harried glance at the back door, where Brad escaped. So he's not infallible; that thought put them on even ground.

Chapter Five

She'd made good time. As she glanced at the clock it only took two hours to scrub every pot, load the dishwasher, running it twice, but that was after she'd soaked and scraped off the dried food. *Did he have to dirty every dish in the house?*

Trevor was a different story; she'd never seen a child so happy to play alone. Katy tried twice to share her dolly and even picked up one of his toy cars and played beside him on the carpet. He'd ignored her, until she'd picked up the green car he lined up in straight line across the coffee table. He screamed a high pitched, shrill cry as if he'd been hurt; Katy of course, starting crying and dropped the car. Trevor, without looking at her, grabbed the car and put it back in its specific spot, in line. Except now, he was making a "whop, whop" sound. Emily hugged Katy and took her in the kitchen, then set her up with her Dolly away from Trevor. Emily asked Trevor what was wrong and asked him not to scream but to use his words. He ignored her. She'd need to talk to Brad; this seemed odd for a child to act this way. Maybe he had abandonment issues. And she pondered that while she cleaned and searched the sparse pantry for something edible to feed everyone for lunch.

* * * *

Emily was stirring the soup on the stove when someone knocked on the front door. She turned off the propane, and hurried to the door, glancing at Trevor and Katy watching *Dora* on the big screen TV; actually Katy sat on the sofa and watched, Trevor was bouncing on both feet two inches from the TV screen.

Emily opened the door to a short guy wearing a brown hat. "Delivery for Brad Friessen."

"He's out back, do you need a signature?"

"Yes, ma'am, but you can sign for him if you swear he lives here and you'll give it to him." The guy chomped on a piece of gum and grinned. Guess that was his sense of humor.

Emily signed for the package and closed the door. A loud crash and what sounded like glass shattering echoed from the kitchen.

"Oh shit!" Emily dropped the box and hustled across the worn wooden floor. Katy stood in the archway wide eyed.

"Mama, Trevor bad." Katy pointed to the tiny little dark haired boy wearing blue cotton pants and a striped T-shirt, barefoot, sitting in an orange, sticky puddle beside an open fridge door. The lower plastic side bar stuck out like a sore thumb and dangled to the floor. Jars and containers scattered the floor. Chunks of glass and pickles surrounded Trevor. "Trevor don't move."

"What the hell's going on in here?" The back door clattered and Brad stomped into the kitchen, brushed past Emily, bent over and picked up his wet boy, moving him out of the mess.

"Stay there." His deep, smoky voice was sharp as he cast an accusatory glance at Emily.

"Weren't you watching him, how in the hell did this happen?"

Trevor tried to step into the puddle of orange juice, flapping his arms and yelling "da, da, da." Over and over.

"Dammit, you're going to cut yourself." Brad picked up Trevor and moved him over by Katy who stood quiet and unsure in the doorway. Big pools filled Katy's eyes. She looked ready to cry.

"Brad a delivery guy brought you a package, I signed

for it. Trevor was in front of the TV. I just turned my back for a second."

The cream-colored walls seemed to vibrate as the tension thickened the air. Katy burst into tears and Brad ran his large callused fingers, the hands of a working man, through his hair, irritated. He ground his teeth with his tight, strong jaw. His Adam's apple bobbed. Then he sighed and threw his hands in the air, as Emily picked up Katy.

He let out a weary laugh and something softened as those magnificent eyes connected with her.

"Well let's clean this up." Brad reached for a roll of paper towel on a shelf at the back door. He ripped off sheets and dropped them onto the puddled juice.

Emily kissed the top of Katy's head and wiped her tears. "Watch *Dora* and let me clean up this mess. I'll come and get you." Katy clung when Emily tried to get her to sit on the sofa. But she appeased her with her dolly and was able to slip away. Trevor was a different story. He was making a "whop, whop" noise as he swayed back and forth just inches from the chunks of glass Brad scrambled to pick-up.

"Why don't I take Trevor and get him cleaned up." She didn't wait for a reply but squatted down in front of the child. He was whimpering in his juice-covered pants, making a different noise now, "whee, whee, whee" over and over again, as he played with his fingers. "Actually, Brad I don't know where his room is. If you could point the way to the bathroom and his room, I'll get him changed into some clean clothes."

It took Emily a moment to realize Brad stopped cleaning up the mess and was watching her with a look that resembled confusion, or maybe he didn't understand what she'd asked. Then he dumped a wad of soggy paper towels into a black garbage bag, and stood to his full height. He gestured toward the back of the kitchen, where there were a set of stairs by the back door.

"Just up those stairs, first door on your right is the bathroom, Trevor's room's beside it on the left."

Emily hesitated in front of the boy. Not in fear, but wondered what his reaction would be toward her. She could feel the heat from his father burning into her back. Clearly, she was center stage.

"Come Trevor let's get you cleaned up." She waited, holding her breath for him to freak out. She didn't want that to happen in front of Brad, she was nervous enough as it was. Trevor was still agitated and he whimpered when Emily reached under his arms and picked him up. Trevor wouldn't look at her but he did wrap his tiny baby-fat little arms around her neck and his wet legs around her waist. Okay so far so good. Emily stopped in the archway. "Katy, come with Mommy."

Emily walked with a sureness up the wooden stairs, Katy right behind her.

Chapter Six

Emily sat Trevor on the long discolored marble counter beside the bathroom sink. Katy perched on a small stool by the toilet. The bathroom was a large, modern bathroom with a soaker tub, lots of cupboards and room for dressing. Emily reached for a burgundy washcloth from one of the cupboards and turned on the tap until the water warmed. She soaked the terry cloth, wrung it out, grabbing Trevor's leg every time he squirmed, and gently wiped his hands, and then his face. "Okay Trevor, stand-up. Let's get you out of these wet clothes."

Katy, her two-year-old bright-eyed angel, looked up. Trevor didn't, instead he jammed the edge of the washcloth in his mouth and chewed. Those pale blue eyes held no recognition to her or anything she said. They appeared glassy unresponsive. "What's wrong with you, Trevor?" Emily snapped her fingers. He didn't even flinch, much less look up.

"Lift your arms." She helped him to stand on the counter but then he reached fitfully for the damp washcloth she pulled from his mouth. And he shrieked. Emily pulled off his shirt and gave it back. He shoved it back in his mouth. Content for the moment suckling away, Emily hurried, cleaning him up.

She carried Trevor the way a mother does, resting on her hip, across the carpeted hall to a child's large bedroom which held a toddler's racing car bed and nightstand with a horsey lamp. There was also a tall mahogany, six-drawer highboy and a toy shelf filled with cars, stuffed toys and children's books. Emily rummaged through the top two drawers until she found another long sleeve, dark blue cotton shirt with matching sweatpants and a pair of socks. She had no trouble pulling the shirt over his head and helping him to step into his pants; he was so focused on chewing on that rag. But when she tried to put on the white cotton socks, he threw the washcloth at Emily and whined a high pitch squeal as he pushed away her hands, kicking his feet against her legs. "Okay, so socks are not going to happen today. We'll leave those for now." Maybe that was why he'd been barefoot.

He calmed down when Emily put the socks back in the drawer. Trevor raced for the discarded washcloth again jamming it in his mouth. "I'm not going to fight with you, Trevor. Keep the washcloth for now. Come on, Katy. Let's go downstairs. This time she carried Katy and held Trevor's hand down the back steps to the kitchen. Trevor never looked up, the way you expect a child to do with a tiny smile or fleeting look connecting in that personal way of non-verbal communication. Trevor focused on the spindle railing and his hand as he dragged it over each groove all the way to the bottom step.

The screen door squealed and slapped against the wood frame. A stocky man about medium height wearing a green plaid loggers coat stalked in. Dirt caked his cowboy boots. He yanked down the brim of his black baseball cap, tufts of dark hair sticking out, and wore what must have been several days' worth of black stubble on his round cheeks. "Hey boss, what do you want to do about the spring hay? You still want to order more from Harley? We can't wait much longer. We only got enough for another few days."

"Ah crap." Brad glanced over his shoulder but didn't get up from where he was crouched down in form fitting jeans, showcasing the perfect set of buns, before an open fridge. He snapped the lower bar back. The floor was now clean and a black garbage bag tucked against the cupboard. Trevor pulled his hand free and raced past the other man. "Eeegg, eeegg," he screamed over and over, gesturing wildly to the fridge.

Brad shut the door and Trevor slapped the shiny white door again and again.

Brad suddenly appeared tired as he let out a heavy sigh. "What do you want? Is it juice?" The thick tension buckled the air in this large square kitchen. Trying to figure out what this child wanted was exhausting and Emily just stared.

The strange man, who now stood beside Emily, rested his large, dirty hands on his hips.

Brad ignored both of them and grabbed Trevor's arm, "Come here." He pulled open the fridge door and Trevor practically dove in for the carton of eggs. His dad lifted him with one arm and pulled him out, closing the door. "No way, how about a cookie?"

"Brad, lunch is almost ready. I just need to reheat the soup. Everything was ready before your box came. Oh sorry, I dropped it by the door." Brad put Trevor down and he once again raced to the fridge and tried to pull it open, screeching at the top of his lungs. This kid was out of control. Brad scooped Trevor up and took a box of chocolate chip cookies out of the cupboard. Jackpot! Trevor stopped flailing and screaming, long enough to greedily cram a cookie into his mouth.

"Uh sorry, at least he's quiet and you can get lunch out."

Emily firmed her lips and crossed her arms. He gave in to this kid, talk about reinforcing bad behavior. But now wasn't the time. She hurried to the stove and flicked on the burner, heating up the pot of soup.

Brad ignored her and spoke with the large man in the kitchen. "Emily how long until lunch is ready?"

She didn't turn around. "Five minutes."

Chapter Seven

Three days after that hellish first day, Emily moved into Brad's house.

She slid closed the glass closet door in her new bedroom—the one beside the main bathroom, which was beside Brad's master bedroom at the top of the stairs. Katy had fallen asleep across her Irish green duvet on her small double bed, clutching her Dora doll and her faded blue baby blanket.

Just this morning Emily discovered this house was built by Brad's grandfather in the 40's. This three thousand square foot, two story home boasted five large bedrooms. Emily's room was freshly painted an off white, with light beige carpeting and a large picture window overlooking the horse paddock and pasture with a lovely view of the distant mountains. Trevor's room was across the hall. Katy's was right beside Trevor's, which left one large bedroom at the end of the hall filled with boxes and furnishings.

When Emily issued notice to her landlord that she was moving, even with the short notice, they'd wished her well. Gina had been true to her word. Gina, Fred, their two teenage boys and what was possibly half the neighborhood packed and moved Emily to the ranch in three days. Katy appeared happy and unruffled, even after the tense first day.

Emily wandered across the hall into Katy's room. She ran her hand over the floral duvet covering Katy's white princess bed. The winnie the pooh lamp sat on the nicked night table. She meant to refinish it many times, but life continued to get in the way.

Emily peeked in on Katy who was the vision of a sleeping angel. It had been an exhausting morning and with all the changes this week and now moving to a new house, it was no surprise after she'd rubbed her eyes, Katy'd crawled up on Emily's bed and fallen asleep. Emily used her fingers to brush back her hair that had slid in front of her eyes. No matter how many times she tied her straight hair back today, it continued to free itself. Now using her fingers, Emily smoothed her hair back and tied it once again into a loose ponytail. She released a heavy sign as she slumped against the door frame, and an overwhelming sensation smothered her as if she'd just come up for air. All because of this whirlwind change, which resulted in her herculean approach to disassemble and pack up an entire house, start a new job and relocate all within a few days. Most of Emily's belongings, including the furniture Bob didn't take, were stored in one of the heated outbuildings behind the barn.

The top stair creaked; she swung around so fast she whacked her elbow on the doorjamb. "Oh."

"Sorry I didn't mean to scare you. Did you hurt yourself?"

"No, I'm fine." Her face must have been crimson, standing in the doorway to her bedroom. Why was this bothering her? And why wouldn't he look away with those intense, dark eyes? Seconds passed before Brad cleared his throat.

"Getting settled in okay?" He shoved his hands in his front pockets, a man who guarded his emotions with a control resembling something hard and mechanical. But the flicker of concern shading his eyes was genuine. Emily liked to think she could pick up any sense of falseness from a person. But she couldn't read this guy. He was too complex.

"I think so." Emily cleared her throat.

His face brightened when he looked over her head. She turned to see what he found so intriguing. "It's been a hectic day for us all I think; hopefully she'll sleep a while." His smile faded. He was standing really close. Her heart thudded. Could he hear it?

She needed to move but he blocked the way. Swallowing the lump, she tucked the wisps of hair that had, once again, escaped the ponytail behind her ears. She dropped her eyes to the floor, a motion that helped her steady her nerves. *Change the subject.* "I should start dinner, it's getting late."

He brushed his hand on her shoulder. Heat flickered. He pulled back as if he'd been burned. Then his jaw hardened as he stepped back, shoving his hands in his pockets again. "Mrs. Haske started something in the crock pot, when she was here this morning to get Trevor, so no need. You finish getting settled."

Her tongue felt thick and she didn't trust herself to speak. She nodded.

"I need to go get Trevor." He hesitated as if needing to say more, but didn't. He hurried down the stairs.

"Brad, I almost forgot ... sorry, do you have a minute?" She cringed at her inability to put together two intelligent words. *Did I stammer?*

He stopped halfway down and turned back. "Yes, Emily." How did he do that? Even the sound of her name sounded like music to her ears. When she didn't respond, he raised his eyebrow to hurry her along. *Okay speak girl.* "Um, I kind of assumed some things; sorry, what I'm trying to say is I just need to clarify some things."

He braced his hand against the wall. He appeared to tense as he stood straighter. She was really mucking this up.

"You're here to look after my boy and cook." Whoa, she'd need a pair of tweezers to remove the stinger from his sharp clipped tone.

"Oh, I know that. But I wanted to talk about getting groceries and the laundry. I'll do Trevor's. And did you want me to do your laundry too? I mean we really didn't talk about all those details. I just want to know for sure…" Emily let her words drop off at the odd expression on his face. He dropped his hand and glanced away. He chuckled as he walked back up the steps. Emily didn't know what to do so she backed up until she bumped the wall.

"Lady, you surprise me. And very few do. No, I can do my own laundry, but thank you. You look after the kids and the cooking and I'll give you money to get groceries, and if you don't mind doing Trevor's laundry, I'd really appreciate it. Fair enough?"

"That's more than fair, Brad. Thank you."

"Mrs. Haske will come a couple times a week to do the cleaning. If you need help with something, you just need to ask. Sorry I snapped. Okay?"

"Okay." She smiled at the encouragement.

"I've got to go." He talked as he hurried down the stairs.

Even though the house was warm, Emily crossed her arms and trembled as she stood alone in the silence, listening to his familiar walk, the click of the door and the sound of his truck.

Chapter Eight

Right after breakfast Emily hustled out the door with Katy, Trevor and a mile long grocery list. Brad, being true to his word, provided her with plenty of cash. She'd made good time through the store and both Katy and Trevor had been on their best behavior. Except standing in line for more than five minutes became a problem, Trevor wanted out of the cart and tried to climb over himself. He yelled when Emily tried to make him sit. So she lifted him out but he then tried to crawl under the cart and ride on the bottom rack. Emily grabbed his legs and he screamed, his arms flailing. Then he threw his shoe, smacking the cashier dead center in her forehead with a pervading thud—it was one of life's most horrifically embarrassing frozen moments in time. The grumpy cashier became hostile and called security. It wasn't just one security guard who showed up but two stern faced, out of shape, middle aged guys who looked like wanna-be cops. While Emily struggled to calm Trevor, who flailed in her arms, and Katy gripped her sleeve whimpering, one of the guards issued her a stern warning to control her child. They didn't do it nicely and pull her aside; they did it in front of all the other shoppers. And Emily still needed to pay.

By the time, she loaded all the groceries in her van, with Trevor and Katy buckled in their car seats both munching on the crackers she'd piled in their laps, her insides were trembling. She worried if, in fact, her picture was now plastered in the store with each cashier with bold black lettering "BEWARE OF THIS CUSTOMER" underneath it.

By the time Emily got home, Mary Haske was already

there. While Emily hauled in the groceries, Mary settled the children in front of the television. Mary was a robust seventy-year-old grey haired woman who wore bifocals and had a grandmotherly smile that warmed Emily's heart.

While Emily put away the groceries, Trevor squealed in a voice sounding exactly like *Arthur*—the cartoon program blaring to life on the TV. When she peaked around the corner, he was bouncing and swaying in front of the TV. Katy was snuggled with her baby blanket on the sofa.

"Would you join me for a cup of tea, my dear." Mary filled a yellow flowered teapot with hot water. "Come sit down."

"Thanks, Mary."

Mary set a tray with milk and sugar and carried it to the oak kitchen table that had been freshly scrubbed. "Sit down while you can, you're going to spend most of the day on your feet, so may as well take advantage of some down time."

Emily accepted the hot mug of tea but waved off the milk and sugar. "Mrs. Haske..."

"Mary, please, I insist. Dear Brad, bless his heart, can't seem to shake the formality. He's called me that since he could first talk."

Emily was drawn into the genuine motherly affection of this woman. "Mary, Brad told me you live down the road and he's known you his whole life."

"His mom and I are old friends, saw that boy in his diapers. We're a small community here. You'll find out. We help out our neighbors. I live down the road on a small ten-acre parcel; it's all that's left of the 50 acres Herman sold off to Brad's daddy. Lived here my whole married life, my Herman, God rest his soul, we were married fifty years when he passed on a few years back. He brought me here from the big city of Spokane. I was a city girl who knew nothing about farming and what it takes to live off the land. He was patient and I cried a lot of tears, packed my bags to leave more times than I can count. I was a silly young thing." Mary smiled warmly.

Emily turned in her chair, so she could see the kids. Actually, her gut ached as she worried what Trevor would do next. "Oh they're just fine, your little angel there seems quite comfortable with Trevor."

"Yes, she's a good girl."

Mary wrapped her hands around her mug as if she needed to warm her hands. She gazed into it, as if needing to say something, but couldn't quite find the words.

"Brad's real special to me. He owns a lot of land here, Emily, almost five hundred acres. His daddy started buying up the land in these parts when families were approached by developers. He didn't want a bunch of small acreages and city slickers moving out here. And Brad has stayed true to his daddy's ways. He's a farmer, he works the land, raises cattle and hay, has dairy cows and he's one of the few around here who's stayed away from all those antibiotics and growth hormones. He's got a good head for business. Smart when the smaller farmers went under. Brad's expanded until he's become the largest dairy producer on this side of the peninsula. What I'm saying to you is he's not good at tending the home. I'm glad he hired you."

"Thank you, I am too." They both laughed, but her frankness about Brad gave her a deeper insight into the fallibility of this difficult man.

"Now I shouldn't be telling you this, but Brad and his two brothers were a wild bunch growing up. One night the sheriff showed up with all three of them in the back of his car. His daddy sure was mad. After that, he worked them pretty hard. Said if they had all this free time to get in trouble, well he'd find more productive ways to direct that energy. And boy, did he. All the farm grunt work was done by his boys, all summer. He didn't need to hire no help that year." They both laughed at the picture that presented.

"Emily, you know, Brad had quite a time finding someone for this job. It was awful. Women apply, they come out, work a few days, see Trevor and one of his spells and they'd leave. And I can see that same look in your eyes."

Emily met those wise, glassy eyes straight on. "There is something wrong with that child. In the store today I didn't know what to do. He went ballistic. Threw his shoe, it hit the cashier and then security was called…" she dropped her face into hands as her stomach pitched, reliving that awful moment.

Mary gripped her forearm. "Brad should have been straight up with you. I've seen some things. Taken him to the store and he'd pee in the middle of the food aisle. There're colors like orange and yellow that he'll yell and scream if sees them. Even the smell of certain perfumed laundry soaps can send him in tailspin. I don't know what to tell you, Emily. I just don't know about these things. In my day, we'd give the child a hard whack on the bottom to straighten him out."

The knowing look Mary fixed on her confirmed her suspicion of this astute woman. "He doesn't know anything's wrong with Trevor, does he?"

Mary threw her hands up. "I raised five young'uns, some kids are high spirited. But Trevor's not quite right. Brad may know deep down, but he's been struggling for a while to just get through day and night."

Emily couldn't fight the urge, even though she knew it wasn't her place to ask. "What about Trevor's mother, what happened to her, didn't she help?"

"Nah, that girl was selfish. A baby didn't fit her lifestyle. The best thing that ever happened to Brad was the day she left. Hurt him bad and changed him overnight."

Her mouth ached; she didn't know how to ask *how'd it change him? What was he like before?* Those questions remained unspoken, locked inside.

Mary finished her tea, and then got up and rinsed her cup in the freshly scrubbed sink before putting the cup in the dishwasher. "Keep Brad out of the kitchen. He's the worst cook and wouldn't know how to put together a proper meal."

Emily figured that much out. The first day when she went to the cupboards, the fridge and freezer, she saw nothing but prepackaged foods, TV dinners and lots of canned ready-to-go meals. Easy and absolutely zero nutritional value. Except the one saving grace, two freezers on the back porch filled with homegrown beef.

Mary lingered for a few hours, showing Emily where things were stored in the house. The chicken coop behind the house, where she could collect eggs, normally one of the hired hands would look after it, but in case they got busy, she'd know what to do.

Emily carried Trevor through the twenty-stall horse barn, with individual turnouts, a hot wash rack, separate hay storage, an outdoor riding ring, a poultry barn for meat birds and the dairy barn. There were several other outbuildings Emily had no idea what they were for. There were, what looked to be, hundreds of cattle grazing in the field with calves dogging their mommies. The sky appeared bluer, larger; so did the pristine untouched forest and the picturesque mountains in the background. It was invigorating, and a lot of responsibility for a man to carry. Maybe that's why Mary showed her around, to give Emily this outside view of how complex a man Brad was. She knew that she'd only skimmed the surface of his life and his responsibilities.

Chapter Nine

Katy became cranky and wanted up. Trevor whined a "whee, whee" sound sure to escalate into a full-blown meltdown so Mary and Emily hustled back to the house. Time had slipped away. Although Mary had provided Emily with loads of information, it had thrown her schedule off. Not that she'd hammered one down yet, but she had a pretty good outline and the only saving grace was the men went to town for lunch.

Now as the kitchen clock mounted on the wall by the table ticked closer to four, she scrambled, grateful the kids were occupied in front of the big screen TV again with their baby blankets, watching *Treehouse*, a children's television station.

Emily grabbed two pounds of butcher wrapped hamburger from one of the large freezers by the back porch and started browning it in a large frying pan. Pulling out the macaroni and canned tomatoes, she hurried to set the table until the meat was cooked enough to add the other ingredients. Just as she assembled the entire casserole, she heard footsteps, the men's deep voices laughing and joking and someone stomped in the back door. She stole a glance over her shoulder as Brad entered the kitchen, alone. He stopped cold and quirked his lips in a teasing way she'd never seen before. Emily glanced down to see what he found so amusing and she nearly tripped over the big black garbage bag propped up beside the fridge. While cooking dinner, cleaning out the fridge somehow found its way onto her list.

"Wow, you wasted no time putting some order into this well-neglected kitchen."

Emily warmed. She was so unsure of her footing around Brad. He could turn on a dime. She needed to distract herself, so she turned back to the stove. But he didn't take the hint; instead, she could feel his heat as he came up behind her. Flustered she wondered if she'd overstepped. "I cleaned out your fridge, I'm not sure how long some of the stuff was in there but I don't think it's edible. And if it's all the same to you, I'd rather just toss it than take a chance." She found the nerve to turn around and face him and willed her shaking hand holding the wooden spoon to stop.

With a twinkle in his eye, he lifted the spoon she was holding and set it down beside the stove. "For safety, just in case you decide to knock me over the head for the mess I left you."

Huh, who the heck was this guy?

"Anyway you're probably right. Mac's been helping out in here, afraid we're not much good in the kitchen. The guys quite often eat here too. Did I mention that?"

"You did. I'm not sure if I made enough tonight. How much do they eat?" Her palms were sweating.

"Relax, they're not coming tonight; they're headed into town as we speak."

Emily was relieved at least for that reprieve, now maybe there'd be leftovers for lunch. "Um, I wanted to talk to you about something that happened today at the store."

"Did I give you enough money?" He frowned.

"Yes, yes you did. It's not that." Oh, boy, how was she going to tell him? "When…" A thunk sounding as if something heavy hit the floor had Brad rushing into the living room, Emily right behind him.

The potted spider plant that was on an entry table lay on its side with dirt spilling out. Trevor was barefoot, dancing in the soil, with a fistful of dirt he was about to shove in his mouth. Brad yanked his hand down and snatched him up. "Oh you little shit." Emily covered her mouth, afraid of Brad's rising temper. But he shook his head and firmed his lips as he turned to Emily. "Sorry it slipped. Not a good spot for the plant Emily, you've got a two year old, I'm surprised you put it so low."

Now this was her fault? *Oh no, I don't think so.* She crossed her arms and took a step forward. "I didn't put it there. And Katy would never pull a plant off the table. And it's been a really busy day. I haven't had time to go through and childproof this house for whatever Trevor can grab and pull down."

Brad's cheeks tinted a subtle pink. She'd hit a nerve. "Okay, I'm sorry. I'll get him cleaned up. Do you want to sweep this up?"

"I'll clean up. Then dinner's ready." She turned her back. Proud she'd said what she did. By the time she tidied up, Brad had Trevor cleaned, changed and deposited back in the living room beside his toy box where Katy was playing with her baby dolls.

"Mmm, smells good." Brad said as he strode to the backdoor, where a rung of a half dozen coat hooks lined the whitewashed wall, and he draped his tan barn coat over one.

Emily put dinner on the table. When she glanced up, Brad was staring at her with such softness, it shot off a fizz of bubbles in her tummy much like a can of soda pop when you first crack it open. He cleared his throat and cocked his head toward the overstuffed black garbage bag. Brad wrinkled his nose as he sidled up to the offensive bag. "I better take it out. Come on, I'll show you where we keep the garbage out back."

Brad tied the two ends of the black garbage bag and hefted it as if it weighed nothing more than a feather. Emily followed to the back porch, but they both stopped in the doorway of the living room. Trevor was stuck in his own world, barefoot and pants-less again, driving his toy cars over a cloth fringe on the coffee table, patting it down then repeating the exact same pattern.

"Oh look at that, he's playing cars with your Katy."

Emily didn't look up at Brad; what she saw was Katy playing with her Dolly, cuddling her blanket and rubbing her eyes. They were sharing space. When she looked up at Brad, he grinned in a way Emily wasn't so sure was joy.

"We better hurry, we're entering the witching hour and something else could land on the floor."

The kitchen clock ticked five. Emily hurried behind Brad to the back porch, where Brad dropped the bag in one of the large black cans, leaning against the side of the house. "Make sure you secure the top down so bears and raccoons can't get in it. That is a mess I don't want to be cleaning up in the morning."

He was abrupt; the change from laughter to serious, all business, was so fast, Emily felt the foolish warm good-all-over glow he put there earlier wiped away. "I will."

He gestured to the door, "Dinner ready?"

Let me get the kids and we can eat."

They walked back in to whining, jumping and the patter of little feet running circles on the hardwood floor.

"The witching hour, huh?" His lips twitched as he glanced down at Emily. "I'll get washed up."

The most unpredictable man sauntered upstairs, how different a man he was from Bob. A nuisance really, Bob, was on Gina's color-coded list, to reorganize Emily's life, of things to handle. Emily sighed. "Katy, Trevor dinner."

Chapter Ten

Emily didn't bring up the incident with Trevor at the market. She kicked herself for days after, for holding onto it. But every time she looked at Brad, she realized there was some hidden fear he didn't want to know. She watched Trevor. She tried to play with him but he wasn't quite right. When he wacked his head on the corner of a wall hard enough to leave a sizeable goose egg, he simply rubbed his head and went back to his cars. The latest trip to the grocery store had him running his hand over the conveyor belt at the checkout; Emily couldn't get him to stop. Little things would set him off into a full-blown meltdown where he'd throw himself to the ground kicking and screaming—pulling him away from the television or his cars if he was lining them up.

If someone new he didn't know came to visit, he'd climb all over them and then wrap himself around their legs. Brad yanked him off the nice lady who showed up with business papers for him to sign. It was embarrassing and Brad had apologized profusely after he yelled at Trevor.

Emily scoured the internet when the kids napped—when Trevor slept. There were times, days, he just wouldn't sleep. She researched his symptoms and what consistently popped up was either mercury poisoning or autism.

Emily needed to find the courage to sit Brad down, and talk with him. Trevor needed help and Emily worried each time she took Trevor out to a store; whether he'd have a public meltdown, if he'd scream and flail. The only thing she could do is pick him up and hurry back to the van with Katy, trying to ignore the hard judgmental glares from strangers. Was she hurting the kid, or just a bad mother? They didn't say it out loud. They didn't have to.

Chapter Eleven

He's an asshole, a thorn in her side, which now began to fester. Why the hell wouldn't the jerk grow some balls and play nice? Sheep were more likely to grow wings before that idiot, who she was unfortunately still married to, decided to become a responsible man. That would best describe all the separation legalities with Bob. He'd left everything for Emily to look after, no surprise there. That's what he did the entire time they were married. All the phone calls, the landlord and the bills he began to challenge were all her responsibility. As her new lawyer, Peter Murphy, said, he was bitter. Even the petty refusal of allowing Emily any part of the damage deposit, which the landlord was still refunding, even with the short notice, only because the house was snatched up by another family. Even though Bob was not paying full child support and no maintenance for Emily, refused to clean the house and handle any of the details for the disconnect services, he still expected all the money. What a piece of work. You hear stories from other women of how nasty their ex's turn when the couples split up. Emily couldn't quite grasp, couldn't wrap her head around, the fact that she'd awakened and realized someone she'd once loved, and thought she knew, had turned into a monster. So to expedite everything, she'd endorsed the entire check over to Bob, refusing to fight over yet one more detail, even though Gina told her not to do it. But Emily didn't want to fight. She had too much on her plate, including caring for an unpredictable child who wasn't even hers.

Her lawyer, Peter, a short, balding man with round

glasses and an overbite, filed the necessary paperwork for legal separation and custody of Katy. Bob hired nobody. He was just being an ass. Visitation, Emily was pleased he'd agreed to every other weekend.

One Tuesday during Emily's third week, Katy and Trevor were seated at the table, their almond butter sandwiches cut up for them, when the telephone rang. Brad wandered in the back door at the same time. He snatched the receiver from the wall phone.

"Hello… Yeah she's right here. It's for you Em."

He passed her the old phone with the long cord, "Hello, this is Emily."

"Emily this won't take long but I need to say my peace." Of all times for Bob's mother to call and how'd she get the number? Emily closed her eyes wondering if the universe would be kind right at this moment and disconnect phone service. Brad draped his tan jacket over the back of the chair. He dished up a small bowl of chicken soup for both kids from the pot in the middle of the table. "Ah Nina, this isn't a good time. It's lunchtime. Can I call you back later?"

"No Emily. I promise this won't take long. I'm so disappointed in you. You just didn't try to hold that marriage together and Katy's the one who's going to pay the price for this mid-life crisis of yours. Bob's worked so hard for you and you appreciate nothing he's ever done for you."

Nina had one of those high grating voices that carried through a phone, the kind everyone in the room could hear. Emily felt shamed when Brad glanced up. Would this make him think less of her? Of course, it didn't look good.

"Look Nina, this is inappropriate for you to be calling here. The relationship with your son did not include you."

"How dare you speak to me like that?"

Trevor started banging a spoon and repeating, "Eeg, eeg, eeg," over and over. Katy, now finished playing with her sandwich, was unsettled and trying to get out of her chair.

"I gotta go."

"Emily I have more to say."

Brad leaned over Trevor. He watched Emily in his hard difficult way. Then he circled his hand in the air to wrap it up. So she turned away, lowering her shaky voice "No, you're done and I'm going to ask you not to call here again." Emily's hand was shaking when she hung up. She pressed her forehead against the wall, taking a deep breath before she turned. She jumped. Brad was right behind her. She never heard him approach. *He's mad.*

"Um, Brad that was..."

"We'll talk after lunch."

Every nerve in her body tightened. Her stomach became unsteady. She forced herself into mommy role, sitting down, feeding the kids and wiping up after Trevor dumped his soup. Long, awkward and Emily couldn't choke down one bite.

After lunch, Emily washed the dishes, taking longer with the chore than she normally did. Brad must have known as he appeared beside her and poured himself a cup of coffee from the full pot beside the stove.

"Put a show on for the kids, it's time to talk. Coffee?"

She looked up into a face that gave nothing away. "Sure." Oh crap, here we go.

Emily popped in a DVD; one of the *Winnie the Pooh* movies Trevor loved and would watch for hours. Katy, wrapped in her baby blanket, popped her thumb in her mouth. She'd probably fall asleep before it was half over.

Emily stepped back into the kitchen. Brad was seated at the head of the table, with a cup of coffee. A second cup in a matching blue floral mug was sitting in the spot right beside him.

Tears burned the back of her eyes. She blinked hard, refusing to allow one tear to fall. She wanted to kick herself for this weepy reaction. She wasn't one of those women who cried at a drop of a hat. She was stronger than that.

His face softened as she sat. She couldn't look at him. Her hands trembled, so she placed them in her lap.

"What's going on?" There was kindness in his voice.

"I'm so sorry." She whispered looking into the eyes of a man filled with so much power and passion, it poured from his eyes. He gave her all his attention. "Why are you sorry, did you do something wrong?"

Emily blinked. "Actually, no I didn't. That was my soon to be ex-mother-in-law on the phone."

"You don't have a good relationship with her?"

"No. She pretty much blames me for ending my marriage to Bob."

"Your ex, he knows you're here?"

"Yeah, he knows. Listen Brad, we never talked about my personal life, but I can assure you it won't affect us here. I'm pretty sure she won't call back again."

"Emily, she hassled you here, in my home. And that's my business. If she calls again and gives you a hard time, I'll handle it." He reached out and touched her hand, a touch that was so tender and full of support, Emily would swear her heart skipped a beat.

"I'll be filing for divorce soon. He doesn't have the backbone to cause trouble. It's easier for him to let me handle everything. He's a mama's boy; forgot to cut the apron strings, as you can tell by the phone call." She tried to make light of her pain, but closed her eyes when he winced at her humiliation.

"I'm sorry Em, if you ever need help with him, let me know. I have to get back to work."

She nodded, fearing her voice would crack if she answered. She stood up when he did and reached for his cup to clear the table. But he stopped her with a soft touch to her arm. And that's all it took for the tears to fall, so much for holding it together. Brad did the unexpected; he ran his hand over her shoulder and pulled her into his strong arms. Arms she was sure could cushion and protect her from every harsh bite reality dished out. An unsettling feeling considering she worked for him. "I'm so sorry. I didn't mean to fall apart."

He must have sensed her embarrassment as he allowed his arms to drop. He stepped back and shoved his chair in with his boot. "That's a lot of hurt you're hanging onto. Suppose you start at the beginning and fill me in."

He slid out her chair. "Sit down." He pulled his chair out, so he faced her when he sat.

"Look, he's just a jerk. He's self-absorbed and thinks of no one but himself. I'm just angry because I didn't see it. He went to work, brought in a paycheck. I was to look after everything else, pay the bills and care for Katy and the house. If something needed fixed, I did it. He refused to give me a break; even slipping out to the store to buy groceries when he was home became a fight if I wouldn't take Katy with me. There was no relationship between me and Bob. I mean he worked in Olympia and commuted; the first thing he did when he walked in, most nights, is call his mother. It bothered me but, as the distance grew between us, I started seeing him as he really was, a stranger who I no longer loved. I felt resentment and tension rose between us to the point where we no longer sat in a room together. There was no peace, no communication and his mother became the third person in our marriage. He shared everything going on his life with her through his nightly phone calls. That's how I found out what was going on with him, by overhearing him on the phone.

Brad leaned forward resting his hand on the table beside Emily. "You listen to me; no real man would put that entire load on a woman's shoulders. That's bullshit, Em. He sounds like nothing but a little boy, not a man.

"Is he supporting your Katy, sending you money?"

Her face heated "Yes, some."

"There are minimum guidelines for child support, is he meeting them?"

She couldn't look him in the eye. She'd asked for very little. "No."

"No? Do you not have a lawyer?"

"I have a lawyer, who's already lectured me, on how I let him off the hook. But I want this over, the easiest way possible. I may be a fool for that. And he can't afford much." What she didn't say was he'd probably bought himself a new car or a new entertainment system. He was worse with money than her.

His brows furrowed. He leaned closer. "He's an asshole, that's what he is."

"Brad, that's not all. I've been reading some research online lately about some unusual symptoms in children. I read about a mother whose child would scream and shout and flail his arms during a Christmas lineup. And all she could do was carry the young child out. He wouldn't play with other children. Noises and scents would set the child off in uncontrollable fits. The behavior was odd and the child wouldn't talk to other people."

"You do a great job, Em. If you need any help or have any problems with your ex, or his mother, you come to me, you hear me? I know his kind, and I know how to deal with him." He tapped the table with his fingers.

Did he hear anything she said? Maybe she was too vague. But then he reached out and slid his fingers down her cheek, then pulled back as if caught doing something he shouldn't. Brad jumped out of his chair so fast Emily wondered if his chair would tip. But he gave it a shove, balling his hands into a fist. Then he grabbed his coat off the chair and faced her. "I meant what I said, Em. I'm a man of my word."

A difficult man walked out the door. One who was hiding his feelings, his thoughts. A man she'd need to be careful with. Keep both eyes open; this man had the ability to cloud her good judgment. Except a thought surfaced in that moment as she listened to the gravel crunch beneath his feet; what it would feel like to be loved and protected by a man like Brad?

Chapter Twelve

Emily was positive Brad had convinced himself nothing was wrong with Trevor. After the glimpse she'd given Brad into some of the research she'd done, research similar to Trevor's symptoms, Brad should have clued in. How much clearer did she need to be when it was obvious there was something wrong with the child? He should recognize the similarities, shouldn't he?

From what she read of Trevor's symptoms, routine was essential. It didn't take a rocket scientist to figure out Trevor's day needed to be structured. He ignored Katy, not deliberately; he'd slip away into his own world to do the oddest things. Restack utensils, boxes and cans in the cupboard over and over. He'd play with the DVD player, shoving a movie in and out over and over. She knew Brad saw that much. She'd seen the odd look come over him when he thought she wasn't watching.

Emily began to notice patterns. One full-blown meltdown came about after he'd consumed a big bowl of ice cream; on the floor, kicking, screaming and flailing his arms all because he couldn't wear his blue pants because they were in the dirty clothes. She researched diet and read the suggestions. Many suggested they can't digest gluten and dairy and both have a big impact on behaviors.

It was time to talk to Brad. She hadn't pushed. But how do you tell a parent, who doesn't see it? He'd be angry, but it would be worse if she said nothing.

Emily waited until she'd bathed and put the kids to bed. She breathed deep as her chest suddenly felt as if a hundred-pound weight pressed against it. She paused in the shadows and listened. The soft glow from Trevor's nightlight shone on the wall at the top of the stairs. Emily could see Brad on the front porch, leaning against the solid white post. He was always outside. From the little she knew of him he wasn't happy unless he was outside. Now as the sun dipped low in the sky, the bright orange and pink glow was the perfect vision before bed. The door squeaked when she pushed it open. Emily pulled the brown sweater she grabbed from the hook around her shoulders. It was cool this time of night.

"Do you have time to talk to me?"

He smiled warmly. "I always have time for you Emily."

"Can we sit down?" She fisted her hands in her sweater, how could she be sweating, it wasn't warm enough.

"Sure."

Emily chose the second rattan chair with the bright blue flowers. She didn't need to look up to know when he sat next to her in the matching chair or that she had his full attention.

"You're not okay. Something happened?"

Truth or dare. *Stop stalling.*

"I don't know how to say this, so I'm just going to say it."

The man could change in an instant. All the warmth and support fled, replaced with something dark and ready to snap. The momentary change made her afraid.

"So you've decided to leave. I should have known better. Why?"

Her mouth gaped. The man jumped to conclusions faster than changing the station on TV. "I'm not leaving, where would you get that idea?"

He threw his hands up, squinting. "Then what is it? Your ex again?"

"No, it's nothing like that. Brad, you know how much time I've been spending with Trevor?"

He relaxed a bit and leaned back in his chair, but she

could still feel him wound up tighter than a steel coil. "Hmm, mmm."

"Okay I just need to say this. You know how you keep getting after Trevor when he does something like dump over a plant and play in the dirt, or the way he latched onto that lady like a human leech?"

He brushed his hand in the air to dismiss her words. "Come on, Emily, he's just a boy, doing little boy things. Don't worry about it. Girls are different, they're easier, just ask my mother."

He truly didn't see anything was wrong. "Trevor doesn't talk, he avoids eye contact, sits lost in his own world and uses a one word vocabulary of maybe fifty words. He has full-blown tantrums on the floor, pounding and screaming. And I don't know what's going to set him off. Could be the wrong food, something was moved or a stranger comes to visit. Trips to stores are a nightmare and my anxiety level goes through the roof because I'm anticipating what he's going to do. He's urinated on the floor in the middle of the grocery store; he had a meltdown in the check out lane and runs his fingers over the conveyor belt where you put your food during checkout. Storekeepers get mad. If I grab his hand to get him to stop, he might scream. Depends on the day, what he's eaten and what's happened before we get to the store. I never know what will set him off." Brad tilted his head, tapped his forefinger against his lips. "You can't reason with him. And the way he stares, he doesn't appear to understand. He plays alone and will not play with Katy no matter how much we try; he moves away if she invades his space. I turn the television on; he loves it. It's like he's consumed by it and even then, he can't sit still. He'll stand in front it jumping, laughing and giggling, engrossed in the rainbow of colors flashing over the screen. I'm betting if you took Trevor to a family gathering or big social event, it'd most likely be a nightmare. His behavior's odd. People get weirded out because they don't know what to do. And I'm pretty sure he picks up on everyone's anxiety. There are safety issues with Trevor beyond the scope of a typical three year old. I always worry while in town if Trevor will dart out into the street. He doesn't recognize cars, traffic or even people around him. He touched the hot stove last week and burned his finger. He never cried; no reaction. Brad, I started researching his symptoms. The internet is full of information and what I discovered were symptoms of autism.

Brad rose and paced, running his fingers through his hair.

"Autistic children are not all the same, they have different symptoms. I've read about therapy for autistic children—therapy tailored for each individual child."

Even in this dim light, Emily glimpsed the color rising in his cheeks. Brad wasn't just pacing and she could feel the adrenaline cut through the space between them. "I need some air."

"Brad, wait!"

"No Em, back off." He kept going, down the stairs toward the barn, as she could almost feel the rage burning through him.

He knew. She'd gotten through. Now the real work begins.

Chapter Thirteen

Bright red numbers flashed 4:39 a.m. on the bedside clock. The rooster crowed. She heard a rustling coming from downstairs. Emily slipped out of bed, pulled on her brown housecoat, the one she kept draped at the foot of her bed. Guided by the hall nightlight, Emily tiptoed to the stairs.

A silhouette of light trickled from the kitchen.

Emily held the cedar handrail as she crept barefoot down the stairs. Brad held the glass carafe from the coffee maker as he fumbled for the coffee in the cupboard. He reeked of booze and wore the same brown plaid shirt from yesterday. Dark stubble covered his cheeks, his chin. His short hair stuck up clumps and tufts. She touched his hand and gently took the carafe. He stared straight ahead, and then turned like a man defeated and walked like the living dead to the table and sat in his chair. He stuck out his heavy work boots, coated with mud. Emily spied the trail he'd tracked from the back door through the kitchen.

Emily scooped coffee into the basket, poured water in the coffee maker and turned it on. What could she say to ease his turmoil? When enough coffee filled the pot, Emily poured out two cups, adding milk and sugar to his. He never looked up when she placed his mug in front of him. Emily pulled out a chair beside him. She sat and scooted closer to the table. She gazed into her coffee, searching for some miracle answer but one wouldn't appear.

Brad didn't move, nor did he reach for his coffee. He leaned forward resting his arms on the table. His lips trembled. A glossy sheen covered the tiny red lines that appeared like sandpaper in his eyes. Had he slept? She'd say not. Was he drunk? More likely, a poor attempt to anesthetize. His dark brown eyes reached out to her with something that appeared lost and helpless.

"Does Trevor have autism?"

Emily lean over and covered the hand he'd balled into a fist. "I'm so sorry; I didn't know how to tell you. But from what I read, he shows all the symptoms."

"Is it my fault, something I did?"

"Oh God no, Brad. They don't know what causes it. But the numbers are skyrocketing; from what I read, every one in a hundred-fifty children will be diagnosed, and it's higher in boys. Out of every five children diagnosed with autism, four are boys. That's an epidemic, not something you did."

"So now what?"

"You need to get him diagnosed. And you need to start an early intervention therapy right away. I've been emailing a local parents group I found on the internet. They sent loads of information for you, so you know where to start."

"I don't understand what you do." Brad was alone and he was looking to her.

"One of the parents, a mother from a mom's support group I've connected with by email, hired a consultant who is trained specifically in neurological disorders, and has a BCBA and psychology degree for children and adults with autism. The consultant is local, just outside Olympia and she has a proven track record. I don't know all the details of what exactly she does, just the basics. But it's a start."

He watched her close, sobering as he listened.

"She works with the schools putting together a home and school program. She sets goals, creates programs for academics, socialization, peer interaction, language and behavior. She establishes strategies and changes what doesn't work. These kids work hard but, from what I've read, these kids make real progress with the right therapy."

"A mom's group, huh? Well how about that? Women who actually care about their kids."

This time when he looked at her, something inside of him pulled away. You know the feeling you get when someone needs distance. He downed the rest of his coffee that had long since gone cold and scraped back his chair. "I need to go take care of the stock and feed the horses. See you at breakfast." Then he was walking out the back door, snatching his barn coat off the hook on the way, as he strode into the darkness and cold morning while the rooster crowed.

Emily stayed where she was, wondering about his wife, the woman who left, the hurt she caused and the little boy she abandoned. Brad concealed it well, but this morning she saw the damage, like tread marks on his soul.

Chapter Fourteen

Emily loved to spend time in the kitchen, baking and creating meals. Brad needed his animals and the outdoors. The kitchen brought balance to her thoughts and emotions and gave her clarity and peace of mind. She was also a damn good cook. And that wasn't ego. She loved putting together a good meal for her loved ones to enjoy, and for the first time since she could remember, she truly felt needed.

When Mary Haske dropped by this morning to clean, she brought with her two freezer bags of Blackberry's. And mentioned how much Brad loved pie. So what did Emily do, she took the hint and ran with it, baking not one but two Blackberry pies along with a marinated roast for dinner. The aroma alone set Emily's mouth to water.

It had been an exhausting week. Brad scheduled a doctor's appointment after breakfast Monday and began the long, grueling path to obtaining an autism diagnosis. Emily contacted the mothers group and provided Brad with names of a local therapist and private psychologist in Olympia. Brad worked the impossible. In two days, he'd somehow arranged for a speech and language pathologist, and occupational therapist to work with Trevor at the ranch once a week.

Emily grinned like a silly schoolgirl, just thinking of Brad and how dedicated a father he could be. Heat pooled inside her tummy until it ached. "Oh bad idea, girl." And she knew why. He was her boss. She lived under his roof. But he didn't treat her like an employee. He spoke to her like a friend.

They'd developed a nightly routine, similar to spouses,

companions. She'd put the kids to bed; join Brad either outside on the porch or in the living room. They'd talk about their day, their dreams.

Brad planned to expand the ranch. Buy up the land around him, even though now he was one of the largest dairy producers in the area, and raising cattle for beef.

She loved listening to his confident whiskey-filled voice when he holed up in his office, off the living room, making calls to arrange transport for a hundred head of cattle. Then a feed order, next his realtor, a burly bald-headed man named Chuck, to put in an offer on a twenty-acre piece of property on the other side of Mary Haske.

Last night Brad told her the soil on that land was really good and the water pure, clean and plentiful. He'd also mentioned he was waiting for the day Mary put her property up for sale. When she did, he'd make sure it was his. A small parcel, but Mary's husband had been sharp when he'd sold off most of his land. He'd held onto the best piece in this part of the peninsula; holding the water rights to the creek which flowed down to Brad's property.

Emily grabbed the salad out of the fridge. She closed door and nearly dropped the bowl. Trevor stood in the middle of the kitchen barefoot wearing nothing but a saggy disposable diaper, rubbing his eyes. "Oh Trevor, I didn't see you." She could smell the heavy ammonia from his dirty diaper. Emily lifted Trevor up. Instinctively he wrapped his arms around her, as she started up the stairs. Halfway up, the screen door slammed.

"Lunch ready?" Brad's deep, soft voice tugged on her heart as if a line had knotted around it. She walked back down carrying his son.

"Oh man, something smells good." Cliff and Mac strode right behind Brad, both lifting their noses in the air, sniffing.

"It is; I just need to change Trevor and wake up Katy." Emily couldn't erase the smile from her face if she wanted to.

"Need help." Brad yelled behind her as she trotted up the stairs.

"Grab the salad dressing out of the fridge, everything else is ready to go."

"Okay."

Emily pulled off Trevor's diaper and dumped it in the garbage; she helped him into his big boy underwear, a pair of blue sweats and Buzz Light-year T-shirt, leaving him barefoot. Katy wandered into the bathroom, pulled off her own dry diaper and sat on the toilet. Girls were almost self-training. "Lunch's ready. Who's hungry?"

"Me, Mama." Katy pulled up her pink sweats and flushed the toilet; Emily pulled up a stool to the sink, and helped Katy wash her hands.

With the kids, Emily strode back in the kitchen. Cliff and Mac were already sitting at the table, digging into the fresh bread and butter. Brad cut up the roast, while Emily sat Trevor in his chair and Katy in her booster seat, dishing up the kids' food and cutting it into bite size pieces. Emily put a spoon in Trevor's hand, helping him to grip the handle. He still didn't know how to use a spoon or fork. He preferred to eat with his hands. But Emily was relentless, working with him at each meal. In the short time she'd been here, they'd come from Trevor launching his spoon, screaming, to where he now took three or four bites from his spoon before dropping it. Emily would reward him after each successful small step with praise and a gummy bear.

Today, it was as if he'd overcome some obstacle. He took the spoon without fuss or whining. Emily glanced over at Brad. "Did you see that?"

"Great job, Em."

Except when Emily glanced down at Trevor, he now used his other hand to play the table like a piano. That was progress for you, one-step forward and another back. Brad curled his fingers around the back of the empty chair beside him, and pulled it out

"Sit down, Em."

Every time he spoke. His deep, husky drawl was like music, turning her insides all soft and fluttery. Emily sat, very aware of his closeness, becoming a silly schoolgirl every time she passed him a bowl or plate of food and their fingers touched. And each time she looked up, he watched her in a way that was personal.

Trevor tossed his spoon across the table, breaking the magic spell where it clanked and landed beside Cliff's plate. At least it didn't hit him. Last week his spoon hit Mac on the side of the head. Trevor, with his tiny fingers, mushed his potatoes and broccoli between his fingers, cramming a fistful in his mouth.

"No." Emily jumped up and leaned across the table, grabbing the spoon.

"It's all right Emily; he didn't mean nothing by it." Said Cliff in his raspy smokers voice followed by his nervous laugh.

"Actually it's not all right Cliff. Trevor can't learn unless you stay vigilant." Emily wiped the food from Trevor's hand with a dishcloth and put the spoon back in his hand. "Try again." Emily said as she scooped a piece of potato on his spoon, and then let go of his hand. This was a fine line with Trevor. There was only so much hand over hand you could do with him before he'd freak out from being touched.

Trevor scooped up another piece of meat himself and shoved it in his mouth. "Good job Trevor. Eat."

When Emily glanced over at Brad, he was already finishing up his plate, guzzling down the last of his coffee and pushing away from the table—distracted again. The man was such a mystery; the way he changed from hot to cold, a difficult and complex man.

"Great lunch Emily. Cliff, Mac, I'm going to need your help as soon as you're done to move the horses. Don't dawdle."

She'd be a fool to miss the annoyance that dripped

from his sharp words. What the hell happened? Her heart sank a little as Brad went out the back door without a simple glance in her direction. Mac scraped up his plate and Cliff downed his coffee; both pushed away from the table nodding their thanks as they hurried after their boss. Brad teasing and thoughtful one moment, turned quicker than she could snap her fingers, to an irritable one; turning her world upside down, leaving her mystified as to what she'd done. Emily pushed her plate away. Well whatever it was, Emily was sure time scooping up manure would most likely take the edge off whatever bothered him, or so she hoped.

Chapter Fifteen

"You need a spare room that's quiet for therapy. A room to put all the teaching supplies and toys you use only for therapy," Pam, a tall thin lady and mother to a fourteen-year-old autistic boy, said. She'd driven down from Olympia.

"We have lots of room here." Brad had been polite, and maybe a little taken back by this woman who headed the local parents' group. She'd already arranged for her consultant to visit Trevor, to assess and set up programming. She was a doer who could set your head spinning for what she'd accomplish in five minutes.

"Brad, what about the bedroom at the end of the hall upstairs. The one filled with boxes and furniture." A dark shadow fell over his face, his eyes flinched and took on a hardness Emily hadn't seen before.

Emily poked around in there the other day and came across some extremely fashionable woman's clothes, stacked high in the closet. A cedar chest tucked in the corner filled with baby clothes. "I'm sorry, if you'd rather that room not be used, I'm sure something else…"

He cut Emily off. "No. Use the room. I'll have Mac clear it out." He'd shut down and packed away the flash of fury she'd swear had reared its ugly little head. Maybe she imagined it.

Pam was looking at them in a way that said she, too, picked up on a problem. But to her credit, she dropped her eyes and started scribbling notes in her spiral bound notebook. "When the consultant comes to visit, you'll want to have it sorted out. Also, line up some therapists. Tamara will start training after she assesses Trevor."

"But I haven't got a diagnosis for autism yet. Isn't all this a little premature." Brad crossed his arms his face was all business.

"By the time you jump through all the hoops needed to get your kid diagnosed, you'll have wasted precious therapy time. The key is early intervention. The earlier Trevor starts, the best chance he has for a positive outcome. If it's about money…"

"No, we'll start. Money's not an issue if it's what's best for my boy. I'll pay; I don't care what it costs." And so they did. For the next two hours, Emily took notes, distracted the children, and started implementing all Pam's suggestions for help with Trevor.

Chapter Sixteen

The soft lilt of Faith Hill singing *Let Me Let Go,* roused Emily from her sleep. Rolling over, she quickly flicked off the radio before kicking back the soft duvet. Emily was a morning person. But for some reason this morning, she could have yanked the quilt over her head and drifted back to sleep. She didn't, even though thoughts of crawling out into the morning chill curled her toes and wiped away the last of her fairytale dream—her knight swooping in on his white horse and carrying her away.

Emily pulled on her robe over her horsey flannel pajamas and crept into the bathroom for a quick shower. After her shower, Emily crept past Brad's closed door, tying her damp hair back in a ponytail, wearing her sneakers, blue jeans and a light red sweatshirt and tiptoed downstairs. She cranked the heat and listened to the furnace kick in. The floor creaked above her. Brad's up. She made coffee as she listened to the water run upstairs. Brad liked to grab a coffee on his way out the door to feed the animals.

Emily got busy making breakfast, oatmeal in a big pot on the stove. Then hurried to the back porch and pulled out a loaf of bread from one of two freezers for toast. Since Emily started cooking, Cliff and Mac appeared like shirttail relatives for every meal. Brad clomped down the stairs and Emily's palms began to sweat.

"Good morning, Em." Emily forced herself to look up into sleepy eyes that would be a dream to wake up to. Brad cleared his throat and Emily snapped out of her daze, blinking as her face tingled a little on the warm side. Emily looked down and snatched up the wooden spoon. Look somewhere else. Maybe she should've moved. Brad reached around her and took a mug from the cupboard, and then reached around her other side for the pot of coffee that just finished brewing. "Can I pour you one?"

Damn, why'd he have to smell so good? He hovered right in her space and her dratted tongue refused to move *answer the man.* "Yes."

He didn't move and when she looked up, he winked. And curse it all, she was blushing. She couldn't shake the feeling of roses, candlelight and good man to cuddle up with. That was the effect this man had on her. Did he know? Maybe that's why he appeared so amused. Grabbing hold of her senses, she poked him in the ribs to break the spell he cast over her. "Where's my coffee?"

Brad didn't reply. He grinned in a sexy way, showing off his chipped front tooth, which on anyone else would have tarnished their appeal, but not on Brad. On him, it added a sense of mystery making you want to get know everything about him. Brad broke the spell when he grabbed another mug. "Did you sleep okay?" How could a woman ever walk away from the deep velvety caress of his voice?

"Yes I did. I realized this morning, Katy's been sleeping through the night since we've been here. Since being in this house, not once has she woken up in the night."

"Katy wake up a lot in the night?"

"Uh-huh, ever since she was born. I could probably count on one hand the number of times I wasn't awakened in the night." Brad didn't move. She'd have to duck under his arm to get past him.

"You have beautiful eyes, Em."

Heat filled her face and this time, he turned away looking like he was having fun. "I need to feed the cattle." He didn't stop until he reached the door. He paused long enough to down the rest of his coffee, drop the mug on a shelf, grab his coat and stride out the door.

What the hell was that?

Chapter Seventeen

Mary Haske arrived after breakfast. She hung up her light jacket in the hall closet, dressed so neat and tidy for cleaning. Brad had just left to feed the horses. Emily could hear the tractor plowing its way to the fenced off fifteen acres, filled with trees, a meadow and a creek, containing Brad's twenty five horses—a paradise for a horse to live this close to nature, with room to run.

"Emily, why don't you take a break? Go on out for a walk on this beautiful property. I've got Trevor and your little angel; I'll watch them for you."

Emily tossed down the sponge she'd used to wipe the counter. She loved this property, the animals and the horses. "You know what? I will. Thank you."

Emily grabbed a coat of the hook and Mary shooed her out the back door. Emily was halfway across the field, her hands shoved in her pockets when she heard Brad yell. Emily hurried to the fence line. A crop of trees surrounded the tractor and several horses seemed to gather around one spot.

"Brad, is everything all right?" She shouted.

"Rusty broke his leg." Rusty was a twenty-year-old quarter horse appaloosa mix, Brad's horse, the one he always rode. Emily hurried to the gate.

"Emily, grab a couple halters and come in here. Close the gate behind you." Emily grabbed three halters with lead ropes attached from the hooks by the gate and then slipped inside, stepping through the muddy track, puddles and damp brush in her new, white running shoes.

Brad was on the other side of the tractor, a bale of hay in the teeth of the loader, waiting to be dropped in the large feeder. Horses surrounded Brad and Rusty, who stood in a small crop of brush with a few small branches sticking out. The closer she got, she could see the blood seeping from a gash just below his hip. Brad yelled at the small dark Arabian who wouldn't leave Rusty's side.

Emily had to push her way through the horses. "Here, I grabbed three."

Brad took the blue halter and slung it on the Arabian.

"Em, I need you to hold Smoky for me." He handed her the lead rope. "Just pull him back, keep him back until I tell you, I need to get a better look." Brad used a soothing voice as he ran his hand down the horses flank. Blood covered Brad's hand and the horse nickered, a sorrowful sound that squeezed the peace right out of Emily's soul.

"How bad is it?" Smoky yanked on the lead rope and swung his backend around. Emily had to yank a few times on the rope to back him up.

Brad hung his head, took of his hat while he rested his hand lovingly on the Rusty's back. "It's bad. I'm going to have to put him down."

It became one of those moments when the hurt surrounding her felt as if her heart shattered into a hundred pieces. His hand shook as he pulled out his cell phone.

"I need to speak with Doc Vander's, it's Brad Friessen… What the hell? No, this is an emergency. Isn't anyone filling in for him…? Okay, give me his number." Brad ended the call. He didn't face Emily. She could see he was struggling to hold it together, the way a man does who's determined to be strong. He punched in some numbers. "This is Brad Friessen; Doc Vander's office gave me your number. I've got to put my horse down he's got a bad break on his hind leg just above the knee. No, he's stuck in some brush. Three hours? I'm not waiting, and letting my horse suffer for that long. Yah, right, thanks for nothing." Brad hung up and squeezed his phone, shaking his fist in the air.

When he faced Emily, he wouldn't look right at her.

He stared off to the side but she didn't miss the sheen of tears that glossed over his eyes. "The vet's on holidays and the closest vet available is on a call in Olympia and can't get here for three hours. I'm going to have to put him down myself."

Emily didn't know what that meant but she figured Smoky did. As he yanked again, this time getting away, almost dragging Emily with him. He flanked Rusty's side once again, rubbing his nuzzle up and down Rusty's neck, as if to comfort him.

Brad stepped away from Rusty. He took off Smoky's lead rope so he wouldn't trip. "Let him say goodbye."

This time when Brad stepped closer, she could see the agony of what he needed to do. She'd heard stories of putting your animals down, but never experienced such a loss. "Brad, are you sure, can't his leg heal? Can't you just wait till the vet gets here? Can't we do something for him?"

Brad shoved his hand through his hair and tightened his lips to a thin line. Then put his black cowboy hat back on his head. "No Emily, there's nothing I can do. His rear leg's broke, just above the knee, and that gash is a branch that poked right through him. If he was a young horse, maybe surgery could be done. He's too old. It wouldn't be fair to him and he's lost too much blood. It'd be cruel to make him suffer." Brad started around Emily. "I'm going to need you to hold Smoky back when I put him down."

"Where are you going?" Brad didn't turn around.

"To get my gun."

Chapter Eighteen

How did one respond to the reality of what was about to happen. Emily climbed into the tractor while Brad hurried back to the house. The horses knew something. Smoky was nose to nose then side to side with Rusty, as if holding him up. And Rusty, his head drooped as if he knew his time was almost up. The other horses lingered close, about a dozen surrounded Rusty and Smoky, forming a circle of protection. It was magnificent, mesmerizing and heartbreaking to watch this procession. They called out to one another, whinnying and snorting. But she'd no idea what they were thinking.

When Brad hurried back, Cliff trailed behind him, his ratty felt hat pulled down low over his eyes and his plaid jacket buttoned up. He put the lead rope back on Smoky. The horse fought Cliff as he led him away from Rusty.

"Emily, don't look." Brad yelled.

Emily ducked her head and shut her eyes, tears streamed down. She jumped from the shots blast, covered her mouth and couldn't hold back a whimper. She gazed through a film of tears at Brad standing over Rusty, his beloved horse, lying in a heap in the brush. Smoky reared up and snickered in the most agonizing way. The other horses swung their tails but did nothing else, a few of them pulled out a mouthful of straw from the loader. But it was the silence in the trees, in the brush and the meadow, as if the land was guiding home a gentle spirit and mourning the loss of such a kind loyal soul.

Brad lowered his gun, allowing it to dangle from his side. He fisted his other hand and brought it to his mouth. His lips trembled as he swiped away a stray tear with his coat sleeve.

Emily climbed down from the loader. And then Brad was right behind her. His face filled with such sorrow. "I need you to help Cliff after I put the hay in the feeder. Hold the horses back while I dig a hole to bury Rusty."

Her throat tightened, she couldn't get anything out. So could only nod. Brad climbed up and started the tractor, the loud diesel drowned out everything. Emily backed away while Brad drove the thirty feet to the feeder and dropped in the round of hay. He backed away. The horses were so used to the tractor; they walked around it to the feeder. Except for Smoky, a bay mare and a white Percheron, they hovered over Rusty.

"Emily hold Smoky while I grab these other two." Brad shouted just as Mac dashed through the gate.

Smoky yanked on his lead. Emily led him further away. Cliff had halters and lead ropes on the other two horses and moved them back. Brad moved in and used the front of the loader to dig a hole beside Rusty. Mac took the Percheron. Blood covered the ground where the horse lay unmoving. Emily buried her face in Smoky's neck who now stood calmly beside her. It was horrible watching Brad slide the horse into the hole and then bury him. She knew this was life on a farm with animals, but she'd never experienced such loss in her life. How could ranchers and farmers deal with this so calmly? She'd always bought her meat at the supermarket wrapped in plastic. You didn't see the cow or chicken still walking around before slaughter.

Brad touched her arm. "Emily, thanks for your help. Go on back to the house. We're done here."

He took the halter off Smoky. The horse wandered over to the grave and stood. The other horses would eat and then wander over and stand by the grave. Brad jumped back in the tractor yelled orders at Cliff. Emily ran out the gate, tears streaming down her face. She didn't stop until she reached the house. Life moved on; they had no time to grieve. Emily stood on the back step and looked back, the tractor, Cliff, Mac and Brad had already moved on.

Chapter Nineteen

"Eyes looking, Trevor." Emily gestured her hand to the child size chair in front of the kid table set up in the new therapy room upstairs in the larger, fifth bedroom at the far end of the hall.

When Trevor didn't respond but continued to flit around the room barefoot, muttering under his breath some recent line to a *Barney* cartoon, Emily gently touched his arm and guided him to the chair. "Sit down." And he did sit, but then began to rock side to side tipping the chair, which fortunately rapped on thick carpeting, cushioning the noise.

Trevor was out of sorts, and had been since his appointment this morning with Jane, the speech and language pathologist, a short curly-haired red head. From the moment she walked in the living room and sat down on the dark leather sofa, Trevor had performed his monkey routine, climbing on the furniture, the chairs, to the floor on all fours and hooting like an elephant, or was it a dog today? She wasn't sure.

Two others, a man and woman, had accompanied Jane, all part of the diagnostic team to officially diagnose Trevor. One was an intern; a dark haired man with a trimmed beard, which she supposed was to make him appear older, more distinguished, but failed miserably. Instead, he looked like a wet-behind-the-ears twenty-year-old. The other woman was an occupational therapist, scrawny with prematurely gray short-cropped hair. She too was observing. Right after introductions were made and Brad and Emily sat in opposite corners of the living room; it all fell apart. The occupational therapist had accepted the coffee Emily offered and sat quietly, appearing shy and a little nervous, on the couch. Trevor jumped from behind the couch onto her shoulders, and then rolled beside her and tried to crawl onto her lap. Her coffee flew out of her hands landing on the coffee table, which was covered with pamphlets and papers on autism, now coffee soaked. The good thing was the mug didn't break. Emily dashed into the kitchen and grabbed a dishtowel beside the sink, and hurried back to wipe up the puddle now dripping from the table onto the floor. Brad, his hardened face flushed pink, stepped in and yanked Trevor off.

Trevor whined and kicked his heels at Brad. Brad smashed his lips together so tight they formed a fine white line. Emily's stomach turned into one hard knot as she picked up on Brad's obvious stress.

Jane perched on the edge of the leather sofa. Her back ramrod straight dropped her bag on the floor beside her feet, and rested both hands on her jean clad knees. "Put Trevor down, he wasn't harming anyone, and maybe Dad should step out so we can assess him without interference."

Brad froze and Emily's mouth fell open as she crouched on her knees holding the soggy towel, now dripping on her faded blue jeans. Now to Brad's credit, he said nothing. But the fire sparking in his magnetic, stormy eyes said it all to Emily. He was going to blow. Emily struggled to her feet. She needed to say something, anything in his defense.

He looked at her with the same steel hardness he leveled on Jane. "Don't" And of course her heart ached from his hurtful rebuff. She understood now the boundaries she crossed, he wouldn't be defended by a woman. He put Trevor down beside Emily, held up both his hands in a show of surrender, and abruptly left through the kitchen, out the back door, slamming it so hard the lights in the kitchen flashed. The feeling of anger trailing behind him filled the air with a noticeable stench setting Emily's teeth on edge.

Trevor pulled away and bounced back over to the uncomfortable OT, who'd become a magnet for Trevor.

His structure had been changed; he didn't know what was expected of him. Hell neither did Emily, as she gawked like an awkward schoolgirl at these three gangly professionals. Trevor was a magnet; picking up on everyone's anxiety. Hers included. And Katy now yanking on Emily's brown T-shirt began to whine until Emily picked her up.

The two hours Jane and her lackeys stayed seemed like eight. When they finally left, Emily was so wired; it left her muscles and bones physically weary. Lunch was a pathetic ensemble of build your own sandwiches which Brad never showed up for anyway.

After Trevor woke from his late morning nap, Emily worked on some basic receptive skills with Trevor, but now he stopped rocking and slid off the chair onto the floor, as if he were a limp rag doll. Emily scooped Trevor up and sat him in the chair holding tight to his upper arms not allowing him to slip off. "Awesome job Trevor, you sat! Here, you earned this to play with." She handed him the tape measure he was so fond of, he yanked it out and let go while it whizzed closed over and over.

The occupational therapist who'd tagged along with Jane as part of the team this morning, insinuated following through with Lovaas ABA therapy, the therapy provided by the new consultant, would in fact harm Trevor. He needed to be left alone and he'd develop in his own time, naturally, he'd make his own friends as he saw fit. It was a good thing Brad had left.

Emily had been furious and kicked a stuffed animal across the floor after they'd walked out the door. Why couldn't these industry professionals start working together? When would they get with program and all realize this is about the best outcome for Trevor, all autistic kids—check your egos at the door.

Her head pounded as she watched Trevor now scoot across the floor on his knees. Today seemed like the saying, "one-step forward and three back." And where was Brad?

Chapter Twenty

The dinner dishes were washed and put away. Emily scrubbed the kitchen table and counter. The sun dipped below the horizon lighting the sky a beautiful shade of pink and orange. Emily listened at the bottom of the stairs for any rustling from the kids. Nothing—good, they were fast asleep.

Dinner had been quiet and tense, even though Emily made Brad's favorite pork chops. For her, it was just a small effort to ease some of the humiliation he'd experienced this morning. He'd only picked at his dinner. After about ten minutes, he'd pushed his plate away and got up from the table without a backward glance, doing something he never did—leave food on his plate.

Walking to the back door, he paused before opening the door, "I have work to do. Thanks for dinner, Em."

"You're welcome." Then he was gone.

Emily stepped outside onto the front porch. The cool night air nipped through the light brown sweater she'd draped over her shoulders. Sitting on the wooden swing, she rocked back and forth. She lifted her chin toward the sound of crunching gravel. Only Brad sounded so confident and surefooted. Emily caught sight of Brad's outline as he paused right before the steps.

"Nice night, are the kids asleep?"

"Not a peep out of them. It didn't take them long. Join me." She motioned to the chair beside her.

He looked straight at the front door. *He wants to escape, he's embarrassed.* "Please Brad."

He took off his worn cowboy hat and played with the brim in a way so unlike the confident, in control, man

"Okay Em." He strode toward her. Instead of sitting, he rested his booted foot on the chair right beside her, resting his forearm on his knee, and then brushed his hat against his leg as if knocking out all the dust.

Emily took a deep steady breath, and pulled out the elastic tying her hair back, allowing her brown wavy hair to scoop down over her shoulders. It was kind of romantic. When Emily looked up the moon had cast a circle of light around them. Brad reached out and touched a strand of her hair, rubbing it gently between his thumb and fingers. Then he tilted her chin up. Her breath was stuck somewhere around the hard lump jamming her throat. Her heart pounded; he was so close now. He leaned down, closing the awkward gap between them and captured her lips in a sweet, tender kiss, so light, his breath warm. He slid his hand around the back of her neck to her shoulder and lifted her until she stood before him. His hands slid down her back and his arms tightened into an embrace as he traced her lips with his tongue to gain entrance. With a gasp, she opened her mouth allowing him access. He deepened the kiss and pulled her tighter to him. His hands slid farther down her back and cupped her bottom. A possessive, bold move, his desire pressed hard against her. He dropped his arms and backed away, one step, two steps, breaking off the off-the-charts kiss; out of breath, both of them breathing deeply, as if they'd just run a marathon.

"I'm sorry, Em. I've wanted to do that for so long."

She stepped forward reaching up, she touched his cheek. "Please don't stop."

He was so tall. Her head barely reached his shoulders. But that didn't stop her from reaching up and trying to pull his head back down to her, except he wouldn't bend.

"Are you sure, Em? This is what you want?"

His whiskey-colored eyes looked amber in the moonlight. The words stuck in her throat as though lodged in something thick and gooey. Emily swallowed past the hard lump. Her invitation must have been clear because he threaded his fingers through her hair. Gripping the back of her head as he pulled her to him, reclaiming her mouth like it was his right and she was his woman, a possessive familiarity Emily had never experienced. His deep, intense kiss shed all sense of sanity and turned her knees to putty. Brad must have sensed her slipping, and tightened his arms around her waist, holding her hard against him.

She clutched wildly to his shirt and her hands wouldn't stop shaking. Her mind fogged. All she could think about was how great her need for him was—a need stifled for so long; she'd lost all control over the situation. A slight whimper sounded from somewhere deep inside of her. Brad pressed into her, every hard inch of himself. *Oh God, how she wanted this, him.* There was something about this man, and oh yes, he was very much a man, that left her screaming and rejoicing as his tongue danced with hers. Oh my, could this man kiss. Maybe that was why her mind allowed dark doubts to creep in; asking her how he could really want her. *You're just a phase, a momentary distraction. Shut up, stop thinking so much*, she told herself, *just enjoy, and don't start looking for problems.*

He broke off the kiss and leaned down. Opening her bulky sweater, he placed tender kisses down her neck to the row of tiny brown buttons above her breast. He then trailed his hand over her breast, pressing softly as he traced the tender outline of her nipple through her cotton shirt. He didn't stop his sweet torture as he cupped and lifted, running his thumb against the underside of her breasts. He pulled away, reaching down, linked her hand in his and guided her into the house, closing and locking the door behind them. He squeezed her hand and looked down on her with such heat and desire in those powerful whiskey colored eyes, pausing with an open question she clearly understood, "Are you sure this is what you want? Tell me now before this goes any further."

"Yes, I want you." Her voice was husky and filled with desire.

Without another word, he led her up the stairs. Each creak of each step bumped up the beat of her heart, and it threatened to close off all her natural breathing. She didn't know how to handle this because with Brad, there was no question; he was in charge. His whole being stated that fact. He was a poster boy for the very definition of a strong alpha male. She'd wondered if men like him hadn't in fact died off long ago. Now she was so grateful he was here with her leading her into his room, closing the door behind him.

Chapter Twenty-One

Brad braced his wide, working man hand flat against the door and just watched her through his heavy lidded gaze, the open question gone. Studying her now was a predatory man, who damn sure wasn't letting her leave this room, but not in a way that instilled fear in Emily. She felt wanted, special. In this large, stately master bedroom filled with western oil paintings, mahogany furnishings and a large four-poster bed, neatly made with a floral duvet whispering the sensual invitation she longed for.

Hypnotized, Emily faced the bed and stepped closer, touching the soft cotton duvet, absorbing the enormity of this step. Brad's arm slid around her waist and pulled her back into his intense heat. She couldn't turn around if she wanted. The top of her head leaned back against his shoulder and she could feel every well-formed muscle in his chest against her back. He gently caressed her shoulder, his rough hand sliding under her shirt, setting her skin on fire. He lifted her long brown hair and held it up, exposing her long silky skin as he applied tender nips with his teeth in between each gentle kiss down the side of her neck. Emily tilted her head back, a gift to allow him more access.

He tucked her hair over her other shoulder and then trailed the tips of his fingers around the outline of her breasts while unbuttoning her shirt slowly and skillfully, one button at a time, with his other hand. She was weak from the hardness of him pressing into her from behind. It was so erotic, with his height and strength. The heightened passion left her anticipating, exposed and at the same time, feeling safe. He didn't pause or fumble his way when opening her shirt and pulling up her bra to expose her breasts, so smoothly, as if he'd done this a thousand times. He then guided her down a sensual trail, an easy tug here and carefree twist there, massaging her nipple with his thumb, first one, and then the other. She reveled in his warm breath on her neck and shoulders followed by a teasing path his tongue traveled over her exposed shoulder. He was driving her mad and she pulled at the arm anchored around her waist. But she couldn't budge him or make him go faster. He decided what to do and set the pace, which was so like him. He unsnapped her jeans and pulled the zipper down, creating such painful pleasure by inching his hand down through her feminine curls, rubbing her, claiming the prize when he slipped a finger inside of her. She heard a low moan and felt herself spiral up and she lost any semblance of control as he began to move and stroke, in and out. She clutched his arm, lost in an intense burning desire, wanting nothing more than for him to bury himself in her hard and deep. "Please I need you inside me. Now, please, Brad." Shameless, she begged, breathless, tossing her head side to side against his chest.

She felt the soft chuckle against the back of her neck. "Patience, Em, just enjoy."

He slipped off her shirt and bra and finally turned her to face him. She reached up to undo the buttons on his shirt. But her fingers were clumsy and trembled with need. He stopped her by covering her hands with his, as she stood before him naked to the waist. Her breasts displayed and ready for his enjoyment; even after nursing Katy, her breasts remained firm and a proud sumptuous handful.

Brad stepped back, his eyes took on a lazy drunken hue and he undid his buttons, pulled off his shirt, dumping it in a heap on the floor. His chest and shoulders were even better to look at naked than clothed. Reminiscent of a Greek statue: solid pecks, six pack abs with light brown chest hair curling a path down to his navel, before disappearing into the waistband of his jeans. Could it get any better? No way. At least Emily couldn't imagine how. Brad lifted her chin with his finger to meet the wide smile of his cat-like grin.

"Soon."

He reached his hand around to the back of her head and claimed her mouth once again. Deeper this time as his tongue mated with hers. He lifted her leg up over his hip, anchoring her as he pulled her to him and rubbed against her, long, thick and hard pressing into her. She reached for him fumbling with the buttons on his jeans, as he strained against the tight stretched material.

Brad lowered her leg and unfastened his jeans. All the while rubbing his other hand up her thigh, gently squeezing all the way, up to where it joined in the center.

He lowered her onto the floral duvet. Standing over her, he hurried to divest her of her sneakers and socks, pulling off jeans and underwear in one swift motion. She now lay naked before him. She felt the heat of his eyes penetrate every inch of her. He was studying her slim belly, the few stretch marks, the firm thighs, and dark curls at her core. It was instinctive for her to spread her legs open. She wanted him now. But when he moved toward her, he grasped her knees and spread them wide, holding her secure so she couldn't move. He bent down and kissed her where she opened. The sear and jolt electrified her. Emily threw her hand up over her mouth biting down on the meaty flesh to stifle the cry that erupted. He parted her with his fingers and she felt his tongue slide inside.

"Oh my God." Did she whisper or scream, she didn't know. Brad was a man in control. She was completely at his mercy. A place she'd never experienced with a man before, losing control as if she'd slipped over the edge on a wild ride at the fair. She reached out and grasped his short brown hair. Operating on pure instinct, she moved her hips, wanting him now buried deep and hard inside of her. He held her down and it hit her hard and explosively. Rippling through her, a burning intensity that spun and tilted her until she thought she'd come apart. Stifling her scream, she tossed her head from side to side.

She heard it again, in a far distant place, a different cry, not hers. Emily drifted in between bits and pieces of conscious reality away from the heavenly abyss where she floated. Awareness chilled her shaking, limp thighs; she was by no means sated, she needed him.

Her chest heaved as she struggled to catch her breath and she heard it again. A crying child—*Katy*. Brad released her, swearing under his breath as he backed away, running his fingers though his hair. His desire sparked a bitter fire in his eyes. It'd see no relief.

Emily wanted to curse and cry for the moment lost. But her child came first—before her own needs. She rolled and slipped off the bed on shaky legs. She pulled on her shirt and stepped into her jeans. She lowered her eyes to pale blue carpet. Reality could be cruel, like a splash of icy water, uncertain. What now? She held her shirt closed as she hurried to the door, yanked it open and hustled down the hall. Katy sat in the middle of her twin bed, rubbing her eyes, clutching her blue blanket and whimpering. Not a sound from Trevor, however, if she didn't quiet Katy quickly, he'd soon be awake too, and that wouldn't be good. Emily gathered Katy into her arms and kissed away her tears, lifting her up with her blanket and cradled her as she tiptoed across the hall to her room. "Shh, baby girl. Mama's got you, shh."

Katy rested her head on Emily's shoulder. She grasped Emily's open shirt with her tiny fists as her sobbing subsided. Emily walked in a circle and turned to the door. Brad leaned in dressed once again. The expression on his face was odd. Almost strange, one she'd never seen before.

"Is she okay?" His voice was gruff, but full of concern.

She whispered, "Yes. I think she just had a bad dream, she should go right back to sleep." He said nothing, and he didn't move. "You're a good mother, Em. Goodnight. I'll see you in the morning."

Her stomach ached with that awful empty yearning. Tonight with Brad was over now. She craved his touch, but she couldn't will him back as she gazed down at her little girl. The heavy lump in her throat hurt. In the darkness, she stood alone, listening to the soft click of his door. Emily closed her eyes tight, mourning her loss, as she hummed softly, until Katy's breathing evened out and she knew she'd fallen back to sleep.

Instead of putting Katy back in her own bed, Emily tucked her in her bed, watching her peaceful angelic face. Emily slid off her shirt and realized she'd left her bra, underwear, socks, shoes, and sweater strewn on Brad's bedroom floor. Emily winced when cold reality sank in; Brad may've come to his senses. First thing tomorrow, she'd retrieve her things in a walk of shame.

Chapter Twenty-Two

A small hand nudged Emily. But Emily tucked the warm duvet higher under her chin, in her warm cocoon. She struggled to open her sleepy eyes searching out the bedside clock, the red numbers flashed 6:10 a.m. For a moment her heart felt like it expanded two sizes in her chest. She bolted upright, throwing back the covers and jumped from bed. How could she have overslept? She cursed under her breath at her own stupidity; she'd forgotten in her funk of self-pity to turn on her alarm. *You idiot.* She'd never relied on it anyway, as she usually was awake at five a.m. But last night—well—what could she say? Talk about leapfrogging right over moral boundaries.

Emily dressed in yesterday's jeans and pulled on a fresh shirt she yanked from her five-drawer dresser. *Why didn't Brad wake me?*

Emily pushed back her tangled hair and she noticed her door had been pulled closed. And piled on the overstuffed chair beside the door were her shoes, sweater and under things she'd left sprawled on Brad's bedroom floor. Emily groaned as she pressed her hands over both warm cheeks.

"Mama, hungry." Katy bounced on top of the bed in her pink ladybug pajamas.

"Okay, I know Katy, just let me finish."

Emily pulled a brush through her hair, yanking at the tangles a little harder than she needed. Then tied it back and was downstairs with Katy a few minutes later. She plopped Katy on the couch with her baby blanket and flicked on the television. "You watch *Treehouse*, I'll make breakfast."

Emily darted around the corner into the kitchen, slamming into the solid wall of a man's chest. Brad squeezed her shoulders and Emily felt her cheeks burn when she looked up into the mysterious eyes that appeared to brighten in the light of day. "I'm sorry Brad, I overslept, I…"

He rubbed her shoulders in a familiar kind sort of way. "Don't worry, Em. I didn't wake you, I thought you needed the sleep. The coffee's already made. We'll be back, in about half an hour. Is that enough time for you to fix something?"

He was being kind—no generous. And Emily was being a flustered, stuttering idiot unable to jumpstart her tongue. "No… I mean, yes it is. Thanks, sorry." She winced and squeezed her eyes shut. But when she opened them, he hadn't moved even though he dropped his hand and no longer touched her.

He watched her with this magical twinkle sparkling in those all seeing eyes, turning Emily's insides to jelly. She'd no clue to what he was thinking. *Did he regret what happened between them?* That was the worst; she wanted to ask, but was scared of what his answer might be.

Brad ran the back of his hand over her cheek. He paused; he studied, then dropped his hand and strode away. A man with a purpose.

It was instinctive to cover his imprint with her hand.

"Mama, hungry."

Come on girl, back to reality. "Ah Katy, just give me a minute." She rushed to the fridge, and took out two dozen eggs. Kicking the door of the fridge closed behind her. In record time, she'd whipped up scrambled eggs and toast. She was just seating Katy when Brad, Cliff and Mac tromped in the back door, stomping the mud off their boots, discussing the recent feed order for the cattle.

"Good morning, Emily." Mac said and Cliff nodded, as they scraped back their chairs and sat.

Pour the coffee. Take a deep breath. Here we go.

Chapter Twenty-Three

The crazy morning passed in a haze. Katy was down for her afternoon nap. Trevor wouldn't sleep. So while Emily sipped a cup of tea, Trevor ran his cars over the fringed doily on the end table by the sofa, back and forth repeating the same circle over and over.

Her feet ached and she couldn't shake the sense of unease. Even Brad had pulled her aside after lunch, before leaving with the men, and whispered in his sexy confident drawl. "We'll talk tonight."

And my, oh my, when she looked up into his eyes, the heat and meaning was clear. Maybe last night meant something to him too, and she lit up with an easy smile. "Okay." He lingered for a minute longer, until the heated meaning seeped into her stubborn worried head.

The front door squeaked and rattled. Emily jumped, spilling a few drops of her hot tea on the scratched oak. "Shit." She hurried around the corner as she heard the soft click, click of unfamiliar footsteps. Fear climbed in Emily's throat threatened to choke off any sound. She skidded around the corner to grab Trevor and froze. Time went into slow-mo-zone, where everything stopped and her senses were magnified a hundred times. A tall leggy blonde, who could have stepped out of a fashion magazine, strode into the living room. Behind her were two large red suitcases propped inside the door. She was, without a doubt, the most beautiful woman Emily had ever seen. Shapely, thin, curves in all the right places, a body, at one time, Emily would have given her right arm for. She had the most magnificent cat-like blue eyes that took on an icy hue as she stared at Emily, while shedding her expensive white leather coat, and tossed it carelessly over the easy chair. Her tight brown sweater and matching brown corduroys fit her like a second skin, in a tasteful way, except Emily honed in on the salon shaped eyebrows that didn't quite match the fawn blonde hair. Her makeup was a skillful work of art. No contest who the beauty was, this woman, who Emily instinctively knew was Crystal, Brad's wife.

"Who are you and why are you in my house?" Her words were sharp, cruel in a way that made Emily feel like the intruder. The good-looking blonde ran her eyes up and down Emily then looked away, dismissing her.

"My name's Emily, Brad hired me to look after Trevor and…"

The woman cut her off with an impatient wave of her hand. Displaying her meticulous manicured nails, painted a vibrant red, and the large square diamond ring set in white gold on her ring finger.

"So where's the boy?" She asked with no particular interest, an ice princess with no plans to thaw.

Emily couldn't find an intelligent word to say, she opened her mouth, and then shut it. She sought out Trevor, who watched the space between her and this woman, as he held his car and rocked side-to-side making his whoop, whoop noise. Emily dashed to Trevor and squatted down, redirecting him back to his line of cars. "Play with your cars, vroom-vroom, park it here." She scooted around, the icy woman hadn't moved. It appeared she wasn't too keen on coming any closer. "Get him to stop that dreadful racket; I'm going to put my suitcases away. I'd like a cup of coffee. Bring it to me when it's ready, dear."

Emily's back shot up ramrod straight. What unbelievable gall. I mean really, she didn't work for her and she wanted to tell her. But she didn't, and the woman didn't wait around for a response. She climbed the stairs with one suitcase in hand to Brad's room.

Emily choked back the lump wedged in her throat, and her heart ached as if pushed through a meat grinder. She watched in disbelief and she'd swear the floor softened beneath her feet. It took a minute to realize it was Trevor screaming. She turned around as he tossed his car across the room, screeching over and over, "da, da, da, da". Emily gave herself a good dressing down and focused everything she had left on Trevor and calming him down.

She hurried to the TV, popped in a *Peter Pan* movie, one of his favorites, and held him while he flailed his arms until the opening music filled the room. He stopped, pulled away from Emily and stood a few inches from the TV screen, swaying back and forth. Where was Brad? Her head throbbed, beating at the base of her skull. The tension lingering in the room had sunk into her shoulders and her neck, to the point she'd swear her muscles would soon snap. Emily wandered and circled the kitchen. Katy was still asleep, it was impossible to slip out to find Brad. She dialed his cell, but it kept going to voicemail. "Brad, it's Emily. Please call me, it's really important."

Emily wrung her hands. Then forced to kick out her ego, she caved and made coffee. What would Brad do? What was going to happen? What about her and Brad? She gazed up at the ceiling and threw her hands up. The timing of this was unbelievable.

The coffee maker beeped and Emily viewed the dark brew as if were a viper ready to strike. She lifted the pot and filled a pink floral mug, even though the muscles in her arms protested what she was doing. *Don't do it. You're not a servant. Don't let her treat you like this. Dump it down the sink and ignore her. Don't let her treat you like this—stop*. But she didn't listen, she swallowed the heavy, hurtful lump that was chalked full of pride, and climbed the stairs while her heart broke a little more. She knocked softly on Brad's closed door, and waited for the hateful woman on the other side to admit her.

"Come in." The summons was light and airy from a

voice that reeked of confidence. Emily pushed open the door. She didn't seek out this rude intruder, but instead her eyes were glued to the large four-poster bed where less than twenty-four hours she'd lay sprawled naked for Brad. The floral duvet hadn't been neatly made, but tossed in a heap in the middle of the bed, where a large red suitcase lay propped open, clothing strewn everywhere.

Crystal cleared her throat roughly. Emily jerked her head and spilled a few drops of coffee on her worn jeans.

"Here's your coffee." Emily extended the mug and dropped her eyes to the floor.

"Where's the cream and sugar?"

So much for avoiding eye contact. "You didn't say you wanted cream and sugar."

"Oh yes I did, cream and one sugar and not that god-awful artificial sweetener. In the future be sure to remember that while you're working here in my house." The warning Emily picked up had nothing to do with coffee.

With shoulders hunched, Emily slunk down the stairs with the despicable mug, positive she could hear the wheel of fortune grind to a halt and reverse, from good to bad. Panic and worry began licking its way into Emily's mind as she wondered what this meant for Brad, her and the kids.

Chapter Twenty-Four

An absolute nightmare, the rest of the afternoon had been predestined. But it was worse than Emily imagined. Thick tension filled every room in the house. Trevor whined, screamed and repeated over and over the same movie line *shoot the Wendy bird.* He spun on his bum in the middle of the kitchen floor, and then flapped his hands when Emily stopped him from shoving toys in and out of the bottom of the stove.

Katy woke from her nap crying, and even now whimpered as she clung to Emily's food splattered blue jeans, shoving her thumb in her mouth. And to make it worse, Crystal wouldn't stay upstairs. She violated all Emily's spaces, rummaging in Emily's closet, and then Katy's and wandering through every room in the house. She settled finally in Brad's office seated in his deep padded swivel chair, and put her high fashion heeled boots on Brads desk. Her smile reminded Emily of the cat that stole all the milk. An hour later, Crystal retreated back to Brad's bedroom.

At three-thirty, while Emily huddled in a corner of the living room with Trevor and Katy creating a Lego townhouse, Brad stormed in. Hurray, the cavalry's here. She wanted to jump up and throw her arms around her guy; the one she knew would throw this awful woman out. But the dangerous glow that lit his face and could set a barn on fire had Emily hunkering down with the kids. Emily had no desire to be on the receiving end of his wrath.

"She in here!"

Katy practically leapt on Emily's lap. Trevor never

looked up.

Emily wanted him to be her knight in shining armor, to ask how she was. But he had tunnel vision. "She's in your bedroom."

"Take the kids out of the house, now."

Well this wasn't good. Brad stormed up the stairs taking them two at a time, slamming his door so hard the living room windows rattled, shredding all hope of a peaceful and calm resolution. Emily leapt to her feet and bundled Trevor and Katy in their coats and hats. She felt an awful chill climb her back; the same kind when you know there's an intruder. She jumped; Cliff lingered outside the door watching her in an odd way. Emily yanked on her coat collar and shivered. He said nothing as he stuffed his hands in his grimy jeans pockets, rocked on his heels, and then strode away.

Brad was shouting so loud she'd swear the walls shook. Emily lifted Katy and grabbed Trevor's hand, leading them outside to the barn to let them romp in a hay pile. More than an hour had passed and Emily crept in the quiet front door. She expected, no hoped, Crystal would be gone and this nightmare ended. When she opened the hall closet, the door squeaked and so did the floor board upstairs. Stress and fury lingered in the air, vibrated in the walls, the floor and the furniture; the kind that did after a battle swept through.

Her heart pounded as she tiptoed around the corner, except it was darn impossible to keep two tired and hungry kids quiet. "Come sit down, how about *Winnie the Pooh*?" The opening credits flashed across the screen when Crystal sauntered down the stairs, her high-heeled boots clicking on the hard wood. She froze at the base of the stairs. Her mouth gaped at the kids perched on the edge of the leather sofa.

The woman was a menace. She crossed her arms over her chest in such an obtrusive, rude gesture and appeared to challenge Emily. Well, Emily didn't and wasn't going to take the bait. What did the woman expect, for her and the kids to disappear? Newsflash, not going to happen. She strode into the kitchen to start dinner and doing her darnedest to ignore Crystal. It was unmistakable; the clickity, clack that followed. Emily opened the fridge and looked over her shoulder. She couldn't help notice Crystal appeared like a duck out of water in this kitchen. She crossed her arms and surveyed the entire room with something resembling disdain. "Is that your kid?"

Emily squeezed her fists and closed the fridge. *Focus on dinner. Forget she's here.* But that was damned impossible when you had hell's fire burning a hole in your back. Emily yanked open the fridge again, her hands trembled as she lifted out the pot of chicken stew and set it on the stove to warm. She then pulled out salad fixings.

The woman didn't move. And now she tapped her toe as if to remind Emily she expected an answer.

Emily let out a soft sigh. "Katy's in with Trevor." She didn't look up, but stirred the stew, struggling against the urge to cry. While Emily made a salad and set the table, Crystal hovered in such a way Emily was forced to step around her. Crystal circled the table as if counting places. Hah, maybe she wanted to see if there was a place for her. Well there wasn't, and until Brad told her otherwise, she wouldn't. What the hell was this woman still doing here anyway? Why hadn't Brad thrown her out?

Emily had a hundred questions for Brad. She glanced at the clock. Her stomach ached with unease. Where was he? "Excuse me." Emily uttered through a clenched jaw as she attempted to put the hot pot of stew on the table. Just then she heard the men stomp in.

Emily didn't realize she was wringing her hands, nor the doomsday clock nipping at the back of her neck. No one said a word to Crystal. Brad paused, glanced at Crystal, and then moved to his spot at the table. Emily's heart sank to her knees. Robotically, she shuffled to the living room, switched off the television.

"Katy, Trevor, dinner's ready." Emily nearly tripped over her feet; Crystal sat in Emily's seat, next to Brad. Mac and Cliff sat stiffly and averted their eyes. Brad wouldn't look at Emily. His face tinged pink and his cheek twitched. *What the hell is going on?* Emily swallowed the rock stuck in her throat and forced back the tears threatening to burn a hold in her head. She seated Trevor beside Crystal and Katy in her spot.

Emily with her face burning grabbed another plate and cutlery from the cupboard, and stumbled to the backdoor for the extra chair. No one offered to help, and she blinked back those hateful tears. It wasn't until she lifted the damn chair that she heard a chair scrape and footsteps. She knew who it was, but now she was too angry and hurt to be relieved.

"I'll take the chair, Em. Let go." She struggled to hold it together, but a cursed tear slipped out, then another.

"Why?"

He closed his eyes. Maybe that was easier than seeing how much he hurt her. "Let's eat, Em. I just want to eat dinner in peace."

What kind of response was that? Left speechless, she let go of the straight back chair. She swiped away the tears and followed Brad. She scooted in her chair beside Katy and dished up. But instead of eating dinner, Emily knew she'd be eating her heart.

Chapter Twenty-Five

Trevor and Katy whined through dinner, they didn't like the stew. They banged their spoons, Katy played with hers, Trevor screeched "no, no, no, stuff, ick," flinging bits of celery and carrots onto the table.

Katy held out her arms to Emily. "Mama, up." Emily scooped her onto her lap and attempted to feed her off her own plate, but she tightened her lips, nothing was getting in. She couldn't blame her, Emily couldn't swallow a single bite either. For some reason, tonight it tasted like sawdust, sticking in her throat and rumbling her queasy stomach.

Trevor started to make the "whop, whop" noise again, swaying in his chair. He held his gravy-filled spoon up and flung it back and forth, the splatters landing on Crystal's perfectly tailored white blouse. Stress thickened the air. Awkward glances, angry glares. No wonder the kids were off, they were intuitive by nature. They may not know all the gritty details, but they knew their secure stable environment had been threatened.

Crystal dropped her fork with a clatter, "Get him out of here." The abrupt dismissal was cruel. She had no compassion for her child. She wouldn't even look at him; in fact, she leaned away, as if whatever he had, she might somehow catch.

The nasty woman pursed her full lips, which Emily was sure were botoxed, reached for a paper napkin and wiped at the splatter of gravy on her lacy shirtfront. How screwed were this woman's priorities? Emily stared at Brad, positive he'd throw Crystal out now. Brad dropped his fork and wiped his gritty hands over his face. He pushed his plate away and leaned his forearms on the table. He ground his teeth. All feeling appeared to seep out of his hard blue eyes when he nodded toward Emily and flicked his hand for her to leave. Her heart sank down through her toes, burning as if the rug had been ripped from under her. And those dreaded tears burned out the corner of her eyes. Blinking ferociously, Emily picked up Katy and held Trevor's hand. She took them both upstairs, into the bathroom and ran them a warm bath. After she cuddled with Katy and Trevor in his bed, she read to them, several stories to help them all unwind. She'd just started on *Scaredy Squirrel*, when she heard the quick light footsteps bounce up the stairs, and then the rustle of Brad's door as it latched closed. Katy grabbed Emily's shirt and popped her thumb in her mouth. Emily closed the book and let out a heavy sigh. "I think that's enough for tonight." She scooted Trevor under his covers took Katy to her room and tucked her in her bed.

Emily paused for a moment at the top of the stairs before swallowing her pride and slipped downstairs, tension building in the pit of her stomach with each step. What was she walking into? This unknown freaked her out and what she saw had her stumbling a few steps in the archway. The table had been cleared and Brad was putting the last remnants of dinner in the fridge.

He glanced over his shoulder, and gestured awkwardly to her full plate on the counter. "You didn't get to eat. So I left your plate out."

Emily gazed at the plate and wanted to scream at Brad. But nothing would come out of her mouth. So she dropped her eyes to the floor.

"Sorry, Em, today… I know this has to be hard for you." He took a couple awkward steps toward her, before shoving both hands in his front pockets. *Aww, here we go, the cowardly retreat.* Her nose was running again and tears blurred her eyes, but she forced a smile to her shaky lips and used the back of her hand to wipe her nose.

Brad frowned.

"Thanks, I'm not really hungry." Her voice caught and if she didn't do something to busy her hands, her mind, she was going to lose it. So she pulled out the plastic wrap from the middle drawer and neatly covered her plate. She walked around Brad, keeping her eyes down and set the plate in the fridge. Then, in an afterthought, she reminded herself no matter what, she wasn't rude or vindictive. She let out a soft sigh and forced herself to lookup. "Thanks for cleaning up; I know it's my job."

Brad ran his hand down her arm. "Goodnight, Em, I'll be bunking in the spare room in the back of the barn. So you know where I am, if you need anything."

She leaned against the counter and just stared. She wanted to say something intelligent. Just what the hell was going on? But he looked away, the stone wall she'd seen the first day slammed down around him. She wasn't going to get anything out of him. This wasn't fair to her or the kids. He had to know this. And maybe he did; he looked away and left without another word.

The floor creaked. Emily jumped. Crystal was just outside the kitchen, her icy blue eyes filled with a meanness Emily couldn't rightly remember experiencing before. The woman was quite beautiful, except coldness tarnished this beauty queen to something of a cold bitch. What did Brad ever see in her? Had she been lurking in the shadows, spying?

Crystal crossed her arms over her full perky breasts. "We need to establish some ground rules. You, your kid and Trevor can start taking your meals earlier. And make sure the kids stay out of my way. I don't know why Brad would have hired someone with a kid. And just so we're clear, Trevor's my child. I'll decide what's best for him. You'll clear everything you do with Trevor through me first. Are we clear?" She made no attempt to soften her voice, dictating with a heavy hand.

"Now wait, I don't work for you. I was hired by Brad. So until Brad tells me otherwise, I work for him, not you."

Crystal took a cocky step forward, as she flicked her sleek blonde hair over her shoulder. She was taller than Emily by a few inches. She used her height to look down on her with a wicked smile that spiked a chill up Emily's spine.

"Let me make myself clear. Brad's my husband and you'll stay away from him. As for this therapy you started; it stops right now. You can look after Trevor and keep him comfortable. But you'll no longer expose him to that kind of cruelty. I've heard about people like you who're so obsessive, you don't see the long-term damage you're doing emotionally. And you're not doing that to my kid."

Emily's jaw dropped. Why hadn't Brad talked to her? Instead he'd run out the door like a coward. "Crystal, I don't know where you heard that. But that's not true. Trevor has so much potential, how can you give up on him? I've researched this therapy, and he's done so well since he started." Crystal leaned in and bared her teeth. "I don't give a shit what you've researched or brainwashed Brad with. Trevor's my kid, not yours!"

The woman was a hyena and Emily wasn't going to win. Crystal started to leave, but then swung back and stepped toward Emily. "Oh and one more thing. Just so we're clear. This is my home and I'm here to stay. So you are very wrong in your assumption that you answer only to Brad. You work for me and you answer to me. If I have any issues with you, I'll make sure you're bounced out of here so fast you won't have time to pack your things." The floor softened beneath her feet, and her heart squeezed so tight she thought it'd explode right out of her chest. The woman climbed the stairs and slammed Brad's door. What followed was Katy's pitiful wail, and Trevor's shriek.

Chapter Twenty-Six

Over the next few days, the tension in the household became untenable. Brad became scarce. At first, Emily thought he was just busy. Then was sure it was to avoid Crystal. But not so, he avoided eye contact with Emily and slipped out the door every time she entered the room.

Emily ate with the children an hour earlier. She stayed away from Crystal the best she could. But it was hard living in a tension-filled house that seemed like a powder keg about to erupt any moment. The kids became cranky and anxious. Trevor regressed, avoiding all eye contact, eating envelopes, paper and labels any chance he could. And when Crystal left her gold plated pen on the kitchen table, Trevor decorated the living room wall with blue lines, circles and squiggles. Emily was in the kitchen making dinner while Katy and Trevor were supposed to be watching *Arthur* on TV. Crystal's high pitch shriek had Emily dropping the lid on the floor and darting into the living room.

She slid to a stop just as Crystal snatched the pen from Trevor's tiny hands. Emily covered both hands over her mouth. An entire wall would need repainted.

"How could you let him do this? You're supposed to be watching him." Crystal screamed which launched Katy off the sofa to hide behind Emily. Trevor let out a high pitch wail, as he wacked his head with his hand over and over.

Emily picked up Katy when she began to cry. She was scared, of course. Crystal was scaring Emily the way she carried on.

"I was making dinner, Trevor was watching TV and I'm sorry, but sometimes these things happen. That's why it's important to make sure you don't leave things like a pen laying around."

Crystal tossed her hands in the air. "Well, you're going to have to pay for it. The cost to have this repainted by a professional is coming out of your pocket."

"That's not fair. It was your pen you left lying around. Of course, he's going to pick it up and draw on something. He doesn't understand…"

"You were hired to look after him. You're not doing a good enough job, so don't you dare blame your carelessness on me." Crystal marched over to the TV and flicked it off.

"This isn't a play room. From now on the kids need to stay out of the living room." And then the woman sauntered up the stairs.

"Watch *Dora,* Momma." Katy gazed up at Emily.

"No, everyone in the kitchen with me, dinner's almost ready anyway."

****

The days got worse. When Brad came in, he ate and left.

Katy started whining over little things. She didn't like her dolly, the book, Trevor was bugging her.

Crystal treated Emily like a servant, always demanding. Do her laundry, make her tea, coffee, clean her bathroom, make her bed and iron her shirts. And always when Emily was busy with the children. After the second day, Cliff and Mac had stopped coming in for dinner, and last night, Brad didn't show up at all, which had Crystal storming out of the kitchen after eating alone.

Brad never explained to her what happened in his fight with Crystal. He kept his distance from her and Trevor. How could she have been so fooled by this man, believing he had integrity?

The few times she'd seen Brad come in, Crystal was right there. She'd run her hand up his chest or arm and smile in such a seductive way; Emily wanted to knock the grin off her face. The last time, Brad gripped her wrist and pushed it away. And he stared at her with such contempt. None of this made sense.

Emily couldn't sleep. She resented Brad for abandoning her. For not standing up for her —for not being the knight in shining armor she'd believed him to be. Emily could no longer subject Katy to this type of cruelty.

Crystal stopped Trevor's therapy and had taken over the therapy room upstairs.

It was underhanded how it happened. Emily had gone into town with the kids. It wasn't until Emily had slipped upstairs to work with Trevor she discovered everything gone, replaced with unfamiliar boxes and art supplies.

Crystal had appeared as if suddenly conjured up, in her designer jeans and silk blouse, looking as if she stepped off the page of a fashion magazine. "I told you there would be no more therapy." She sauntered around Emily and Trevor into the room, raising her eyebrow as if to accentuate her point. "I've already discussed this matter with Brad."

It had taken Emily over an hour before she was able to track Brad down. He had been out in the north field. She saw him as soon as he cleared the tree line, riding Smoky. He dismounted and passed Smoky to Mac. "Unsaddle him."

She couldn't hold it in, as she clutched Trevor and Katy's hand. "How could you stop Trevor's therapy, move his toys, his therapy programs—everything out. How could you go along with her?" She trembled with the anger, the strain, it was all too much.

Brad bunched his fists and turned away from Emily and allowed a flow of foul curses to break free. The force of the words and the venom in his voice made Emily jump. Then he caught sight of movement by the side of the barn.

Cliff leaned against the barn watching. Brad pounded the dirt as he stormed toward Cliff. "What the fuck do you know about this fucking bullshit and what that bitch did?" He grabbed the man's jacket and shoved him against the barn.

Emily took a step back. She had a pretty good idea, for Brad to use the "F" word, it was a good indication of how pissed off he was. We're talking code level red. Cliff tried to get away. When Brad let go, Cliff stepped back on his narrow long legs, his face paled, holding his hat in hand. His rumpled blonde hair was in bad need of a haircut.

"Uh, your wife made me move the things out. I put them in the storage shed at the back of the barn."

Emily hurried past Cliff and into the barn. She yanked on the wooden doors. Brad covered her hand with his on the door frame. When she looked up to him, she knew he saw the clear pools gathered in the corner of her eyes. He put his hand on her shoulder to stop her. Then he opened the doors wider. There, just inside the doorway piled against the sidewall were the books, toys, teaching material, child's table and chairs.

"I'm sorry, Em, I can't believe she did that, we'll get a room set up in the bunkhouse. There's an empty room in there and it's well away from the house."

She just shook her head. "No, Brad. Trevor is your child. Do you have any idea of what it took to get you to see there was something wrong with Trevor, to get him help? And you let this happen. You can't allow this to happen to Trevor, Brad." To know when you're beaten is not a great feeling. Emily couldn't remember experiencing such a hollow loss. This wasn't her fight and she couldn't take it on. Brad winced, knowing full well she was right. Emily held tight to both kids and strode away with her head high.

She didn't turn around when the wooden doors slammed closed, the clink of the lock as Brad shut away all Trevor's therapy tools. She kept going into the house, Brad on her heels. He brushed passed her and the kids as they shed their coats, taking the stairs two at a time, stomping down the hall to where Crystal was holed up in her newly reclaimed sanctuary, with her easel, paints and sketchbooks. The door slammed shut and an argument raged for twenty minutes, before Brad stormed out, without mention or glance to Emily.

* * * *

On her hand, Emily counted the clear facts. Crystal came home. She was Brad's wife. He'd made his choice and Emily needed to accept it and move on, no matter how much it hurt.

Emily stepped onto the darkened front porch, slipping on her wool brown sweater. Upstairs the kids were asleep and Crystal retired to Brad's room.

Emily leaned against the portico and closed her eyes, absorbing the music from a choir of frogs. Emily removed the barrette in her hair. And ran her fingers through the long silky strands. She let out a weary sigh and wandered to the wicker chair, flopped down into it, leaning back and she allowed the tears to fall. Emily shut her eyes and prayed for help out of this hellish situation. She prayed for guidance, some answer to pop into her head and tell her what to do.

"I wanted to apologize to you. I know it hasn't been easy."

Emily leaped forward and ducked her head swiping away the tears. She didn't hear him creep up. She rummaged her pocket for a Kleenex and blew her nose.

His face was hidden in the shadows, but his voice didn't lie, a man of few words. What did she really know about him, his past? Not much if she was honest with herself. When she looked up the moon flickered in and out of the scattered clouds.

She couldn't talk—she didn't want to make this easy for him. This was his mistake, not hers. So why was she being punished?

"You've handled this badly, Brad." She took a deep breath, to steady her voice. "I can't stay, I'm sorry, but this isn't right. You've not been fair to me and Katy, to Trevor."

Even though it was dark, she could almost feel the heat from his flushed face. He lowered his head and looked away. He blew out a hard breath and sank in the chair beside her. This time he leaned forward and honestly looked at her. He dangled his cowboy hat between his fingers. The sparks—the attraction, would it ever be gone? Even after what he'd done?

"Where will you go?"

This time she didn't try to hide the tears. She was mad at herself for falling for the first man who'd told her everything she wanted to hear. She realized why it hurt so much, even after these hellish few days. She'd still held out hope Brad would see the error of his ways, take a stand and tell her he wouldn't let her go. That he was a fool and she meant something to him, he'd make Crystal leave. But he said none of that. A reality that crumbled the last of the pedestal she'd stuck him on. *Idiot.* The strong, confident, honorable hero she assumed he was dissolved before her eyes. It would be easier to hate him.

"I'll call Gina to see if we can stay with her until I find another job, a place to live. I'm sorry for Trevor. I hope…" Emily's voice shook. Her face was drenched by the tears pouring down her cheeks, a free-fall. Even after what Bob had done to her, abandoning her emotionally, not being there for her, not being the man she wanted, but a little boy. With Brad, this hurt worse. Maybe because of whom she thought he was. The first man she'd really looked up to, depended on, in a way she never thought possible. He had strong values and views on the role of a man and woman. The way he loved and cherished his son, a dependable man who could handle any problem, fix anything, or so she'd come to believe. But she was fooled.

How could she have been so wrong? Not once had he brought up what almost happened between them, their intimacy, what they'd shared. Was it that easy for a man to erase from his mind?

The simple truth of the matter was he'd allowed a spiteful, mean, hurtful woman to walk back into his house and treat Emily, Katy and Trevor horribly. Could he not see how Crystal was hurting her own son—his son?

"You hope what, Em?" Brad reached out and clasped her hand, squeezing tight. Emily wiped her eyes and noticed the sheen of tears gloss his eyes before he looked away.

"I'll call Gina in the morning. See if we can't move tomorrow."

Brad said nothing. He nodded and appeared very much a lost man struggling to stay afloat. Even with his scruffy hair and what appeared to be two days without shaving, it was just like him to be so unbelievably handsome. And he'd never be hers. Well, damn him to hell.

"I'll make sure you're paid up till the end of the month."

It was that damn pride which almost had her refusing. She bit her tongue. No, he owes me. Brad squeezed her hand when she said nothing, and then pulled away. The chair creaked when he stood. She gazed up. He stared off into the darkness, fingering the brim of his hat. Then he placed it on his head and strode off, down the steps, swallowed into darkness. The sound of gravel crunching beneath his boots, each step, cut open the hole in her heart a little wider.

The painful lump in her throat swelled, breaking apart any hope Emily had of not falling apart. Her body, her chest shook as the noisy sob burst out. Tears flowed; she buried her face, covering her mouth, as she wept openly on the porch, no one to comfort her, just the sounds of a broken spirit, echoing in the night.

Chapter Twenty-Seven

Brad wanted to eat out his guts as he walked away. Listening to this kind, loving woman weep so pitifully. He was responsible for her pain. She was a wonderful woman, the best thing to happen to him and Trevor, and she didn't deserve this. But it was better for her to leave. This wasn't her battle and she'd become the target. An innocent he couldn't protect.

It was killing him, this whole twisted, fucked up mess. Brad should have protected himself years ago. Filed for divorce and established through the courts legal custody of Trevor. You know, to make sure every "i" is dotted and every "t" crossed. It was careless on his part, which was so unlike him. In any other area of his life he was shrewd, paid attention to detail and never took anything for granted. So why, in his personal life, hadn't he done that? His five hundred acre ranch had been in his family for two generations. In business, Brad was shrewd and he'd turned this ranch into the successful operation it was now. Although his daddy had done well, Brad took advantage of every opportunity, expanding, landing the dairy contract for the area, was the largest beef producer on the peninsula and haying. He saw opportunities and he took them.

So how'd he manage to allow a woman like Crystal to cuckold him, use his son, his one weakness, against him? *And for what purpose*? Since she'd shown up, he'd been unable to find out what she really wanted. He didn't believe her passionate plea that she wanted to be his wife, a mother to Trevor, she'd had a change of heart and she loved him and needed him. Bullshit.

He'd allowed her to get away with far too much,

including allowing her access to his bank account, their joint account. But this was only one in a long line up of many truly monstrous fuckups. But he'd been a desperate man, drowning in the care of his child. A child, he now knew wasn't quite right.

When Trevor was born, she'd never looked after him. She'd fretted through her entire pregnancy of the baby ruining her body. She was amazing in bed, but she'd never truly been his wife.

Now after years of being gone, she still avoided Trevor, wouldn't touch him, look at him or talk to him. Nothing. So why was she really here?

Well she was up to something. Their big blow up revealed a few things. She knew way too much of his personal business, his current offers to buy more land, his pending development permit to build a big show ring for the horses he was breeding. How'd she find out? Well, once Brad found that leak, he'd plug it and find a way to be rid of her.

As for Emily, just thinking of her sweet innocence and what this must be doing to her pounded the nausea in his stomach. He knew she cared for him and Trevor. She wore her heart on her sleeve, her passion for life and her angelic love for children. She was so beautiful. Her inner radiance reached out to touch whoever was around. Brad leaned against the worn cedar siding on the barn. He squeezed his fists and slapped his hat against his leg. He wanted to hit something. Emily, Katy and Trevor deserved better. Brad slid open the barn door and climbed the ladder into the loft. It was completely dark as he sank down against the wall.

He'd never expected Crystal to return. When she first walked out, he tracked her down in Hawaii. He jumped on the next plane; arrived at the all-inclusive resort where she'd rented a suite. He'd convinced the hotel manager to let him into her suite and he waited for two hours for Crystal to show. Time healed some wounds, but not that.

He'd watched as his wife burst through her hotel room door, giggling, wearing a skimpy green string bikini with some blonde buff young surfer draped and drooling over her. The arrogant prick left after Brad threatened to kick his ass if he touched his wife, and even then, he had to shove the guy a couple times before he stood down. Crystal stared right through Brad, like a cold heartless bitch. She poured herself a glass of red wine. When Brad yanked her suitcase from the closet and started jamming in her clothes, she'd clawed his arms and face, threatening to call security if he didn't leave. She screamed and cried; she never wanted to be a mother and shouted Brad was no fun anymore.

Until then, Brad couldn't see her for what she really was. But she successfully ripped off his tattered blinders. He left, slept in a chair at the airport and hopped on the first plane home. He never tried to find her again. Crystal stayed away. She never called. And Brad did nothing but care for his son, and struggle to get through each day. And that mistake was what Emily and the children paid for now.

Once he was a fool. Never again. This sudden change of heart, Crystal now wanting a marriage, even expecting Brad to return to the bedroom and feigning a deep frantic concern for a child she didn't know—what did she want?

At one time, Brad would have done anything to have her, to keep her. As a young arrogant player, he'd obsessed with having her. Now the only feelings he could summon were contempt and a bone chilling fear when she'd threatened to take Trevor, the first day, during their first of many fights.

Emily filled his dreams at night. She was the type of woman he'd never looked twice at. But now, every part of her small rounded bottom, curvy bust and innocent soft eyes, filled and occupied his every waking moment. He dreamed of running his fingers through her heaps of rich brown hair, with its gentle waves that bounced over her shoulder. Every time he closed his eyes, he'd picture her silky warm and naked, lying under him, her brown eyes shimmering with open desire, an honest love given with no expectations.

When he walked upstairs into his bedroom the afternoon Crystal arrived home, he was bowled over by her brash and bold arrogance. She'd hung all her clothes in his closet, as if she'd never left. She'd raced over to him and threw her arms around his neck, pressing her full breasts against him, "Aren't you happy to see me?"

Brad couldn't believe how good she looked, even as he pried her arms away. Her smile turned bitter. She crossed her arms and coldness filled her pale blue eyes. She accused him of sleeping with Emily, said she was his paid whore. She twisted his feelings, the goodness Emily brought here and tainted it with her own poison.

Crystal knew Brad was attempting to get Trevor diagnosed with autism, that Emily was doing therapy with Trevor.

He still remembered how he grabbed her suitcases, now stored in the back of the closet, and opened them on the bed. He said nothing, but seized her neatly hung clothes and shoved them in her fancy bags. She was a dirty fighter; she clawed at his arm, and then had the nerve to say, "I know you're trying to steal Mary Haske's property. Right out from under her."

Someone had been talking, but not the truth. Brad would never do that to Mary, but he'd be first to buy when she put it on the market. He also knew by Crystal's smile she'd hurt Mary with her lies, twisting the story into something it wasn't. Because Brad hadn't been completely honest with Mary, he'd never told her he was buying up the land around her, he wanted hers, and that his realtor was now watching and waiting for hers to be listed.

"I want a divorce. And I want you out of my house." Brad fisted his hands and had to remind himself no matter what, don't hit her. Keep your hands down.

She laughed a deep seductive, throaty laugh and raised

her palms up as if showing him something. "If you try to divorce me, or throw me out of this house, my lawyer will proceed with action to take Trevor away from you with full custody of the boy. I'll take half of this ranch that's been in your family for two generations."

Crystal now paced around him; a woman with a plan.

"Then I'll subdivide this property, breaking it up and sell it piece by piece."

Brad wondered if the chest pains he was experiencing were just a warning or a heart attack. Because he knew she was right. She'd done her homework. She also knew Brad would pay her to go away, but the ranch was a part of him, taking this prime land and breaking it up would hurt him. But it was the threat of taking Trevor away that would kill him. That threat, she knew, would be enough to keep him in line.

Crystal yanked open the drawer of the bedside table and pulled out her black channel bag. She dug inside and handed him a letter from her lawyer.

Brad hesitated he shoved his hands in his pocket. His chest tightened; he struggled to breath. But he gave in and ripped the papers from her hand. As he read the legalese, a cold sweat beaded his spine. She'd placed Trevor on a list for an institution in California for autistic children. Her lawyer had already begun the paperwork and Trevor hadn't even been diagnosed, citing a long waiting list.

Brad was positive the room took on a slow sick spin, and the floor softened beneath him. He ground his teeth so hard and then roared. Throwing his arms in the air, he backed Crystal into a corner and rammed his fist through the wall above her head. Crystal screamed and ducked. Brad backed away and the papers fell to the floor. His knuckles were scraped and bleeding. He stared at her scrawny neck and pictured his hands wrapped around it, squeezing the life out of this cold heartless bitch. She screamed, and must have seen the threat of murder in his eyes. He blinked then grabbed the crumpled letter at his feet ran down the stairs. Brad flicked open his cell phone and dialed his old friend, and lawyer, Keith Rainer, as he climbed in his truck.

"I need to talk to Keith, this is Brad Friessen."

"I'm sorry Mr. Friessen, Keith's at home sick today. Can I take a message?"

"No, I'll call him at home." He hung up on Keith's secretary and dialed Keith's home number. Brad had grown up with Keith, went to school together, chased girls and, as teenagers, were a nuisance, causing all kinds of typical teenage trouble together.

The phone rang six times before the poor bugger answered. He could barely talk and he sounded like he was so congested. He coughed so hard, Brad would swear he choked up a lung. When Brad told him what happened, he urged him to come over. Thank goodness, he was close. Keith owned a small acreage not far from Brad.

Keith looked like hell, his dark hair sticking up in clumps, a two-day beard, pale with a bright red nose. Jenny, Keith's high school sweetheart, and now his plump, short wife, frowned from the kitchen when Keith led Brad into his home office with a box of Kleenex tucked under his arm. He zipped up his dark blue hoodie and sank down in a brown leather chair, scooting closer to the desk. Brad sat across from him and handed him the letter from Crystal's lawyer. Keith plucked out a few tissues, blew his nose and dumped the wet tissues in a pile on his desk. When he adjusted his gold-rimmed glasses, his blood shot eyes appeared to wither before Brad. "I'm sick; my head's pounding so let's not mince words. You fucked up, Brad. You should have filed for legal separation and full custody of Trevor when Crystal walked out. I told you then."

Keith waved the letter in the air. "I've heard of this guy, Sandy; he's slimy and underhanded. They've created quite the tale. You forced Crystal out of the house when Trevor was a baby, while she struggled in a bottomless pit of sorrow with postpartum depression." Keith flicked the letter with this finger. "This part's my favorite. You hid her child from her and kept her from seeing Trevor. You told her she had no rights and she had to do everything you said, when you said it. Now with Trevor being diagnosed with autism, her only interest is to make sure Trevor's respected for who he is. He was born this way and should be left this way; it's who he is. Also she'll not allow you to experiment with her child, engaging him in a therapy that is cruel, abusive and isolates him."

"Is there a possibility she can win?

"Absolutely." Keith tossed down the letter, grabbed a wad of Kleenex, and blew his stuffed up nose. "So what happened to your hand?

Brad glanced down at the dried blood on his knuckle. He squeezed his fist and winced. "I lost my temper and put my fist threw the wall above the bitch's head."

Keith didn't move, but his bloodshot eyes took on that stern parents look. The one you get when you screwed up big time.

"I know it was stupid, but fuck, look what the conniving bitch is doing."

"You better pull your head out of your ass. I guarantee you right now; if she didn't call the cops, she's taking pictures for her lawyer. And she'll play this up. You're building her case for her."

"She's dragged Emily into this, saying if there is any inappropriate behavior with Emily and she'll take action against me. How does she even know about Emily?"

Keith coughed and leaned back in his seat. He held up the flat of his hand. "Are you involved with this woman?"

Brad's face colored. He fidgeted in the straight back chair. "I hired her to look after Trevor and to cook. But I got to tell you this woman's amazing. She helped me see there was something wrong with Trevor. She researched autism, contacted a parents group and helped me to see his symptoms. She helped me connect with the right people to get him diagnosed and to start intervention. She helped me understand my kid. She fought for Trevor, who's not her kid, and she's taught me not to give up, to advocate, to help Trevor. She showed me the potential and chance my kid has for a bright future. And she has so much love and passion flowing through her veins; I think she's the most beautiful, selfless woman out there." Brad knew he was shouting.

"So you're in love with her. And she works for you. Kind of like the servant and master. You sleeping with her?"

Brad nearly came out of his chair but instead, he slammed his fist down knocking over the pencil holder on the exceptionally neat desk.

Keith calmly picked up the dark green plastic holder, pushed aside a stack of bills, clearing the desk so the only thing on it was his box of tissue. Keith rested his arms on his desktop then glanced at the open door. Frowning, he casually glanced back at Brad. "You always were a player with the ladies all through high school. I watched you when you chased around Crystal, your head shoved so far up your ass you couldn't see how she'd lead you around by the nose hairs. Just so you could have some hot filly hanging off your arm. To you it was just looks, always going for the same type, a blonde bimbo whose only interest was your bank account and their own pretty ass. What the fuck are you doing?"

It was as if a light bulb blinked on and Brad was ashamed. He'd allowed his feeling for Emily to lead him. He'd pushed aside the little voice warning him to leave her alone. But he wanted her and the sparks between them were off the charts. But not in a got-to-get-you-into-bed, purely physical way, like it had been with Crystal. With Emily, it was deeper. Something he'd never experienced, nor thought possible. He wanted something real with her, and right now, he saw it being snatched away. "I don't know anymore."

"Yah, well let me give you a little advice. Whatever

you're doing with this lady, you end it now. You've got enough trouble in your backyard you need to clean up first. Let me paint you a picture. You're standing in front of a judge. Your whole relationship with the lady will be the focus, after of course, you're painted as the abusive violent man who can't control his temper, who threw out a postpartum woman who was terrified of you and your threats and didn't believe she had any rights. And yes, she may have behaved badly, using your money. But she didn't know what to do. You separated her from her baby. Who is also being diagnosed, as we speak, with autism. You don't tell the mother, and she's devastated when she finds out, giving her the strength to stand up to you. Meanwhile back at the farm, you've paid a woman to move in and cook for you, look after Crystal's child and warm your bed at night. She's there at your beck and call, tending to all your needs. But it's not a relationship. She's an employee you pay. Add to that, her small child, who's watching all of this behavior. I hope you're following how this is going to look for a judge. A powerful man with no respect for women—women he has to have on his terms, his way. Get the picture?"

"That is absolute bullshit." Brad shouted again. This time Keith got up and closed the door.

"It's not about the truth, Brad, it's who can put the best spin on the situation. And you're playing right into Crystal and her lawyer's hands."

Brad needed to defend himself—to get Keith to understand the truth. The picture he painted was ugly and not what happened, not really. But he was Emily's boss. And he did almost sleep with her. If Katy hadn't wakened, he would have had Emily in bed and under him, doing all manner of loving with her all night. So really, it was a good thing they were interrupted, no harm done, no regrets. Right? "So now what? What do I do?"

Keith didn't sit. He wandered over to the large window and gazed out at his horses in the paddock, as they grazed on the green grass. "You behave yourself. Stay away from Crystal and Emily. No more hanky panky with the lady. Control your temper. Sleep in another room, preferably not the house. You give Crystal nothing to work with. And I'll file for legal separation, with a motion for divorce and petition the court for sole custody of Trevor. I'll ask the judge to order Crystal out of the house. But this'll take time. And from now on Brad, you call me first before doing any more stupid, hotheaded moves. Because if you raise your hand at Crystal again, she can call the sheriff, have you removed from the property with a restraining order against you. She'll keep Trevor and your property, she can drag this out for years, putting her in a position of power and the judge will throw the book at you."

So as Brad sat alone in the dark, thinking back to that awful day Crystal came home, his gut all mashed up as if shot through a meat grinder. He struggled with his painful decision. If it had just been the ranch, he'd have called Crystal's bluff. But he couldn't gamble with his little boy's future. The innocent little boy he loved more than his next breath.

It was better this way—better Emily left. He could no longer stand by and watch her dragged through the mud. It nearly broke his heart to see her the last few days. He'd done his best to protect her. He'd warned Crystal to leave her alone, even going so far as to bargain with the devil herself. He'd stay away from Emily, but Crystal was to as well. Emily was there to care for Trevor and cook. Crystal made it a point to touch, caress and fling herself at Brad every time Emily walked in. And Brad didn't miss the beaten down look that haunted Emily, crushing her vibrant spirit.

This was all Brad's fault. He'd screwed up. And in the darkness, his back to the rough barn wall, he wept, furious at God in that moment for all the injustices in life, and why it had to be so damn hard.

Chapter Twenty-Eight

A thin wall of clouds filled the morning sky. Emily shoved her hands in her heavy coat pocket as Mac tied a rope to secure her belongings in the back of Brad's pickup truck. Emily's throat and chest ached as if she'd swallowed her heart whole; furious at whatever twisted fate ripped the carpet right from under her. She wanted nothing more than to be loved, deeply. It hurt so much to realize this dream had been flushed right down the toilet. Emily pulled at the hem of her brown coat. Wanting nothing more to hurry and get the hell out of here—and at the same time needing to see Brad one more time.

Emily sensed someone watching her. She glanced up at the white sheer curtain as it fluttered in the closed upstairs window. She could still feel the heat of burning hatred.

This morning as Emily packed, Crystal pranced up the stairs and into Emily's bedroom where Trevor lined up blocks in a straight line, then stacked them in a precise order, while Katy played with her dolly, on the floor.

"Emily, is there anything I can help you with?" Her voice sounded joyfully light. And for a nanosecond, Emily believed there may have been some sincerity in her offer. She smiled to herself; well of course the offer was sincere. After all, Emily, Crystal's obstacle, had been slain and was on her way out the door. What a generous offer to help hurry her out. For all she knew Crystal was planning a party.

"No thank you, I'll be done here shortly. But you're going need to look after Trevor soon." Crystal glanced down at Trevor and her smile slipped. She stepped back, once, twice and stopped in the doorway.

It was hard to tell through all that makeup, but Emily was sure her face paled.

"Okay … sure. I guess I can take him now if you'd like." Crystal shuffled half a step. Then another one, her normally fluent moves became boxlike and jilted. Her hand trembled as she bent over. She pulled away as if she expected Trevor to jump up and bite. "Hello, boy, come here please. She dangled her now stiff hand straight in front of him, and then snapped her fingers. "Trevor, come with Mommy. You can watch some television. Would you like that?" She reached for his hand, the one holding the block. Trevor shrieked and dropped to the floor, rolling on his back and kicking his legs in the air. Crystal jumped back. Trevor then screamed his "whoop whoop" noise over and over again—the one Crystal really hated.

Crystal pressed her back to the door. "Stop that, right now, Trevor. Stop it this instant," she yelled.

Trevor held his hand up in front of his face and banged his blocks with his other hand. Katy scooted on the bed. Emily blew out a long breath as she sank down in front of Trevor.

"Hey, let's build these blocks again, come on sit up." Emily placed a block in Trevor's hand, well aware it could fly across the room.

"Crystal, just leave him for now. I'll bring him down when I'm done." It was the only way to calm Trevor down, get Crystal to leave.

Her mouth gaped as if she wanted to challenge Emily, but something softened her hard unfeeling eyes when she glanced at Trevor, relief maybe, but something else, something real transformed her, for the briefest of moments, into something human. Turning, Crystal left.

After her last bag was zipped, Emily leaned down and hugged Trevor who was calmly playing with his blocks. He went into her arms, ripping open a hollow ache in her heart when he gripped her shirt with his tiny hands, "Trevor, I have to go. I love you." Emily pulled away and held his arms as he stood in front of her, trying to memorize his innocent face, the light freckles and the brown wavy hair, which hadn't been brushed today. His eyes appeared distant, unaware, but his face colored. A boy she'd come to think of as her own, stuck in between two worlds. He sensed something, she knew that much, and maybe he did understand she was leaving.

She held Trevor's tiny hand. "Come on, Katy bug; let's take Trevor to his room."

Emily left Trevor with his cars and fringed place mat on his bedroom floor. He hunkered down and drove each car, one by one, over the fringe, lining them up, patting down the fringe, and started all over again.

Emily found Crystal waiting in the living room flipping through a magazine. "Trevor's upstairs in his room playing cars. You need to go and watch him. Don't leave him unattended." Crystal closed the magazine and set it aside, but Emily didn't miss the way her shoulders tensed. She casually tossed back her hair, uncrossed her legs and rose with all the grace Emily had once longed for.

"Well, good luck to you." She paused for a second on the first step. Maybe she had more to say. Except she glanced up the stairs and then flicked her hand in a casual wave as she climbed, her heals clicking on each step.

Emily, returning her thoughts to the present, turned away from Crystal's bedroom window and took a last look around the house. She took in the sights of the horses grazing in the meadow on the east side of the house, the cattle grazing in the far pasture and all the outbuildings scattering the property. Brad had a thriving business, his life, his land. And that nagging question she'd yet to ask. Why'd he let Crystal stay, when he could have so much?"

When Mac strode around the side of the truck, Emily was buckling Katy in her car seat

"All loaded, you ready to go?"

"Let's go."

She closed Katy's door and she felt Brad, more than she heard his heavy steps crunch through the gravel. Where'd he been all morning? She thought she'd cried her last tear. But the heaviness in her chest threatened to spout another round. She refused to give in, to give him that satisfaction. This was killing her and she refused to make this easy for him. Except when he stepped closer, he appeared to have aged ten years overnight. Deepened lines surrounded his bloodshot eyes—eyes that appeared to have seen no sleep. His shoulders hunched, a man defeated. He yanked down the brim of his black cowboy hat so his face remained in the shadows. He said nothing for what seemed like forever. Even Mac made some excuse and slid away. Emily struggled with a need to make it easier for him. Maybe touch his arm, say it's okay. But it wasn't, so she bit her lower lip, sucking it in to stop herself. *Look away, don't look at him.* But she couldn't, she loved the way he looked, his broad shoulders, the way he filled his snug Levis and the wisdom that was always a part of his warm brown eyes.

He turned his head away and squinted when the sun cut through the clouds. He reached inside his jacket and pulled out a thick envelope. He cleared his gruff throat. "Here, Em."

This somehow made it final. Her lip trembled and tears leaked as she took the envelope. She didn't know where to look, what to do when Brad stepped forward and pulled her against him, where she'd always dreamed to be, in his arms. She buried her face in his chest and her body jerked from the sob she couldn't hold back. She slid her arms around his waist crumpling the envelope as Brad rubbed her back and rested his chin on her head. She breathed him in. How could he smell so good? She wanted to scream at the injustice of being denied a life with Brad and Trevor. *Dammit, Emily, suck it up. You're better than this* His rough fingers brushed away her tears.

"If you need anything, Em, you call me. Do you hear?

You call me and I swear to God, I'll be there."

She wanted to kiss him but fought the urge when he pulled back, and then walked away. She could barely see him through the open floodgate in her eyes as he disappeared around the house.

She wiped her eyes. Emily didn't know what it was that made her look up. But when she did, Crystal was there, watching her in a way that sent a shiver up Emily's spine.

It was time to get the hell out of here. Emily climbed in her van and opened the crushed envelope in her hand. It was filled with cash and a check. But it was the amount that squeezed off Emily's breath, almost a year's pay, or close. Why so much?

She couldn't think about it now, so she stuffed that envelope into her dreaded purse. Mac backed up the truck waiting for her to take lead. Emily pulled in front and headed down the long driveway, saying goodbye to each magnificent tree shading this grand entryway. Emily didn't look back, not once, no matter how tempted. She let out a hard sigh when she hit the main road, wondering when the pain ripping her soul apart would ease, just a little.

* * * *

Brad watched from the side of the barn as Mac followed in the big one ton, with Emily's belongings piled in the back; tied down so nothing would fall out. He had no idea how long he stayed, willing her to return. For the first time, he felt himself drowning in a black inky darkness. What a cruel twist of fate, to finally realize he'd found a woman who could honestly love him not for his pocketbook, but for him. He could do nothing but watch her walk away; out of his life, taking with her everything good, honest and loving. She was the best thing to happen to him and his son, and there wasn't a damn thing he could do about it.

He slammed his fist against the side of the barn.

Dragging in a hard breath, he turned his eyes toward the house. Never before had he hated someone as he did the vile woman he'd once loved. Right now all he could do is bide his time, protect his boy and bury the burning rage filling his gut. He pushed away from the barn and stalked toward the house. War had been declared. And this bitch who turned his life upside down was in for one hell of a battle. He'd be dammed if she won. "Let the games begin." He muttered under his breath as he yanked open the door. "Hey Crystal, you need to get lunch started, Trevor needs to eat." He heard a clatter as if something knocked over upstairs. And Brad chuckled under his breath. "Well, two can play this game, baby."

Chapter Twenty-Nine

Gina and her husband, Fred, lived on the edge of Hoquiam, in a beautiful newer area of large homes, manicured lawns and flower-filled gardens. Even though the homes' styles varied throughout this concrete community, the tan color scheme gave a sense of sameness while driving through it; people either loved or hated it. Gina stood in the middle of the driveway, arms crossed as if ready to take on the devil himself. Her husband traipsed out of the house and waved his large hand as Emily parked on the street in front of the house. Fred, only a few inches taller than Gina, stood behind his wife—a solid, balding man who could stand to shed a few pounds. He was a good, honest and quiet man; a glazier who never had a bad word to say about anyone.

Emily liked him. She glanced at Katy, sound asleep.

"Well, you look like crap." Gina met her halfway down the driveway.

Emily swiped away another of the endless tears that had become a constant flow these last few days. Maybe it was relief or all the anxiety she'd held onto for so long; she snorted. "You have a way with words."

Fred lingered a few steps behind Gina. "Hey, Emily." When he smiled, you knew it was genuine.

"Hi Fred, thanks again for your help. I'm so sorry to be imposing on you guys." Mac climbed out of the truck, the engine idled. "Where should I park?"

Fred walked around Emily. "Back in the driveway, there's a side door to the basement; we'll shove everything in there.

Mac nodded and backed the truck in. Fred yanked

open the front door and shouted. "Lance, Rick, get out here and give us a hand unloading Emily's stuff."

Two gangly teens, with light brown hair that was a little too long, shuffled out of the house.

Moving out of the men's way, Emily stepped onto the neatly manicured grass with Gina. "I really appreciate you and Fred letting us stay here, but I promise you, I'll find us a place quickly, and we'll be out of here in no time. And we won't get underfoot. Katy's really good, you know that."

"I know, I know, would you stop worrying? We'll help you get a place. I've already made up the guest room for you and Katy." Katy whimpered from her car seat. Gina unbuckled her and carried her into the house "Go grab yourself a coffee Emily; I just made a fresh pot."

Emily wandered alone into Gina's large dream kitchen; something like what you'd see plastered on the front of those renovation magazines. She listened to Gina ramble on to Katy, showing her the dusty toys she pulled out of the basement for her to play with. Katy was quiet and silent when Gina wandered back into the kitchen with her.

"So what did Bob say when you told him you were leaving the ranch?"

"Well, brace yourself. He said he knew I couldn't make it on my own. And a few things had to change before he'd allow me to come back."

Gina's mouth dropped. "What?"

"I burst his fantasy bubble really quick. I was in no mood to put up with his bullshit. So I told him I was filing for divorce. He didn't say anything except for me to let him know our new address and phone number. I gave yours and he said nothing. He hung up."

"I cannot believe you were married to that man for all those years. Jesus, Emily, was he always this much of an asshole?"

Emily flinched, wondering at what point she'd allowed her values to compromise. Even with Brad, she had to wonder what the hell was tattooed on her forehead. There had to be a reason she constantly found herself yearning to be loved.

"Sorry, Emily, don't answer that…"

"Gina, where does Emily want her suitcases?" Fred yelled from the back door.

Emily jumped.

"Sit down, I'll take of this. You relax; drink your coffee."

Gina barked orders to Fred and the boys, taking Katy with her outside. Soon the truck started and pulled away. Emily didn't move. She didn't say thank-you, goodbye, or anything. She let Mac slip away as if burying the last part of Brad.

* * * *

The next few weeks left Emily dizzy. She found a small house close to town. Actually, Fred found the small older fixer-upper, belonging to one of his buddies. Fred recruited a few friends to move Emily and Katy. Bob had shown no concern over her plight. He picked Katy up every other weekend for his obligatory visit, but Emily wondered if that was only to hurt Emily because he showed no interest in Katy. But in the next breath, the man offered to take Katy on his "off" weekend to help her out. She was done trying to figure him out.

Emily was down on all fours digging in the front garden when Bob pulled up to the small two-bedroom bungalow. Katy was in the backseat of a shiny red brand new mustang. Emily dropped her trowel in the dirt, wiped her hands on her faded blue jeans. She strode toward Bob as he lifted Katy out of her car seat. Laughing, he lifted Katy high in the air as she giggled and squealed.

Katy snatched her blue blanket from her dad and raced to Emily, demanding to be lifted—an attitude she'd not seen before.

Bob zipped up his dark blue windbreaker and lingered for a minute in front of Emily. "You seem to have done pretty well for yourself, Emily."

Emily firmed her lips and leaned around Bob. "Nice wheels. Are those gold spoked? That must have set you back a lot of money." He just shrugged.

"Well after all, I'm the one having to commute to pick up Katy. I need a decent vehicle."

"A sports car, which I'm guessing is fully loaded. So is that where all the money you can't pay full child support is going?" Katy grabbed Emily's shirt by the collar and twisted. She kissed the top of her head, and plunked her on the ground.

He popped on his sunglasses so Emily couldn't see his eyes. He shrugged and walked away.

"Katy, go and grab your wheelbarrow on the front step." Katy toddled to the step, dropping her blanket and grabbed her green plastic wheelbarrow and started filling it with dirt.

"You know Bob, I let you off easy. You don't even pay the minimum child support set by the state. I've asked nothing for me, and you go out and buy some fancy new sports car and try and bullshit me with this crap of being necessary transportation. Let me guess, you took out another car loan, financing this whole thing?" He didn't stop, but picked up his pace pausing only to open the driver's door. He swallowed hard, climbed in, and squealed his tires as he left.

"Asshole." When Emily turned around, her elderly neighbor, Jim, waved from where he watered his flowerbed in front. Emily's cheeks burned, she waved, ducked her head and hurried inside. "Great show, Emily."

The phone rang just as Emily closed the door. Katy turned on the TV and dragged out her dolls. Emily grabbed the kitchen phone. "Hello."

"I'm looking for Emily Nelson."

"Speaking." She didn't recognize the male voice on

the other end.

"This is Taylor at Banters Farm and Feed. You applied for a part time job in our gardening department?"

"Oh yes." The day after she landed on Gina's doorstep, Gina suggested she apply.

"Well if you're interested, I have a part-time opening two days a week."

She grabbed the back of an envelope and scribbled the details, part time and average pay enough to keep from blowing through Brad's nest egg. With the tiny amount Bob paid each month, she'd have enough if she was careful. She'd need to find a sitter for Katy.

Two days later, Emily started her new job, a menial job, hands in the dirt, but was one she enjoyed which helped take her mind off Brad, instead of thinking of him a hundred times a day.

Emily set out a tray of starter plants, outside the front door.

"Whoo hoo, Emily."

She stumbled and nearly dropped the tray. In disbelief, she watched Crystal climb out of a fancy, brand new Cadillac SUV. What was with all these new vehicles? The woman made a beeline right for her, wearing designer jeans and matching jean jacket, her bright red toenails sticking out the end of her open toe high-heeled shoes. Her lips were painted a bright red, not a blonde hair out of place. She tucked her Gucci purse under her arm and waved her fingers high in the air as if they were long lost kin.

Emily looked right and then left. *Hide.* But the woman cornered her as a cat did a mouse. "Oh Emily, how are you. It's so good to see you." She reached over and touched Emily's arm.

Emily stepped back and bumped the rack of starter plants behind her. "I'm fine." She tried to slip around Crystal. But the woman stepped forward boxing her in.

"Oh Emily, I've got to tell you, Brad and I are doing so good now. It was a little rocky at first, but just the other day he was telling me how glad he is I'm home."

Emily's throat became so dry she thought she'd choke. Crystal smiled brightly, all white gleaming teeth, one of the cover girl photos. "You know Brad had this wonderful idea of renewing our wedding vows. How romantic is that? He's everything I ever wanted in a husband. He's so attentive to my needs. Why he just bought me this brand new Cadillac. He wanted to make sure I was safe and had something decent to drive. So have you talked to Brad lately?"

What the hell? "Ah, no." Emily jammed her hands in her apron pocket. Crystal smiled in a way of the cat who stole the cream.

"Excuse me I really have to get back to work."

Crystal stepped back enough that Emily could squeak past. "Oh yes, of course. I'm done here anyway. This store doesn't really carry the quality, or variety, of perennials the more established stores do." She tossed Emily a high quick wave, as if they'd been friends for years. With her Gucci tucked under her arm, she strode back to her fancy SUV.

"How's Trevor?" Emily stepped closer to the curb.

Crystal's hand froze on the door handle. Maybe two seconds passed before she faced Emily, the smile long gone. "Who?"

Emily crossed her bare arms over her blue T-shirt. "Your son, Brad's son, Trevor. How is he?"

"I know he's my son. And he's not your concern. He's fine—better than fine now." Crystal climbed in and slammed her door. She backed out in such a way, if someone was behind her, she'd have knocked them over. Emily blinked back tears, stung beyond belief at how Brad could be so fickle. To allow this woman into his life, his bed and lavish her with expensive gifts. How could he turn his son, who she believed was the most important thing in his life, over to her? She'd been played. So of course, she questioned all her choices, after all, how sound could her judgment be?

Chapter Thirty

It had been three weeks and two days since she'd last seen Brad—since she moved out of his house. This was Bob's weekend with Katy, and for the first time since then, Emily was at a loss as to what to do. So she cleaned the house, top to bottom, and then wandered to the store to grab dinner and rent a movie.

Emily wandered the junk food aisle. Forget dinner, she needed snacks, chips and dip to go with her movie. She stuffed not one but two bags of the extra salty ripple chips into her basket. She whipped around the corner; positive she had all she needed to assemble a tasty dip, looking down in the basket instead of straight ahead, and was nearly knocked over. Emily stepped back and wondered if she gasped when she gazed into his soft brown eyes. Of course, her stomach started doing all kinds of acrobatic flips. So no, her desire for him hadn't dimmed in the least. He looked fantastic in his snug Levis, buttoned up plaid shirt and faded jean jacket. He wore his black cowboy hat, the one she loved, knew he practically lived in it.

Trevor, her lost little boy, clung to his daddy's hand, chomping on crackers from the open box in Brad's other hand.

"Hi. How are you?" How pitiful was that? She couldn't pretend he meant nothing. So she dropped her eyes as her cheeks heated and she was positive her face was blood red.

"I'm fine, Em, how are you?" She darted a shy glance at Brad and didn't miss the sorrow that seemed to dim the light in his eyes. He seemed older, too. His handsome face seemed deeply marked with heavy lines and shadows. Even the gray dotting his hair seemed heavier.

Emily wanted to jump up and down. How could she be excited and devastated at the same time? "Brad, I … I…"

Brad stuffed the open box of crackers in the rack with the bottled water freeing his hand. He squeezed her shoulder and stepped closer. "Really, Em, I need to know how you are. Is everything okay?"

He didn't look away. In fact, the way he watched her, she'd swear he really cared. "I'm fine." Her voice trembled and she took a breath. "I have a job; I'm working at the gardening store at the edge of town."

"That's the one Taylor Banter owns, right?"

"Yah. He's very nice man."

"I'm glad to hear it. So how do you like working there?"

She glanced away and then back at Brad. "I like it. But then, I like plants and everything to do with dirt and growing things. I thought you knew I was there, after Crystal dropped in. Oh and congratulations; she told me you're planning on renewing your wedding vows." She tried to sound happy for him, she really did, but she ached so bad, the bitterness made her sound like a spiteful old hag. She never could play politics. "Sorry…" She forced a smile that strained her face and then gazed down at Trevor—a little boy she still thought of as hers. He wouldn't look at her. Because he was out of crackers and the box was out of reach, he began his "whoop whoop" rocking back and forth. He was no better. Didn't Brad see that? When she looked back up, Emily needed to step back by the wildness that appeared to seethe from every part of him.

"You saw Crystal. When?" His voice was a little loud; some shoppers turned their heads, stopped and gawked.

"A week ago, you didn't know?"

"No. And where ever would you get the idea I'm renewing vows with Crystal?"

"So you're not renewing your vows?"

He turned his head while he let go of a string of curses under his breath. An elderly lady turned her cart around and went the other way.

"I guess that was for my benefit."

It was natural to touch his arm. "Do you have time for coffee?" She put herself out there, hoping he wouldn't turn her down.

"Sure, there's a coffee house next door."

"Let me pay for this, and we'll go." Emily lifted her basket of snacks, and then waved at his open box of crackers. "Are you going to pay for that?"

"Ah yes, thanks for reminding me." He reached for the box and followed Emily to the checkout. He sat his box in with her groceries and paid for everything. She tried to refuse, but he wouldn't listen, as he handed cash to the cashier.

The overweight, dark haired cashier looked at Emily and then Brad. "I think I'd listen to him, he's bigger than you are. And listen honey, if a man wants to pay for your groceries, let him. I wish one would pay for mine."

An older guy, all gray and hunched, standing in line behind Brad, also piped in. "She's right, just let him pay."

Emily closed her mouth frowned and glanced at Brad who appeared to beam from the backup. Emily lifted her bag of groceries and marched out the door, Brad and Trevor right behind her.

Next door was a small coffee shop. Brad held the door for Emily. She grabbed a booth and placed her grocery bag on the floor. Brad scooted in with Trevor across from Emily. The only other customers in this eight-table coffee shop were an elderly couple chatting at a small round table across the room.

A middle-aged waitress appeared with two menus and a coloring book and crayons for Trevor.

"What can I get you?"

"You want coffee, Em?"

"Sure."

"Two coffees, one cream, and sugar, black for Emily and an apple juice for my boy."

The waitress had a brilliant white teeth smile. She used her finger to flick back her dark bangs, which were a little on the long side. "Do you need a few minutes to look over the menu?"

"No nothing to eat for me. Em?"

Emily handed her menu back to the waitress. "Just coffee, thanks."

The lady frowned but took both menus and scooted away.

Brad reached in his grocery bag and pulled out a handful of crackers for Trevor, and piled them on a paper napkin. Trevor saw only the crackers, and one by one shoved them in his mouth and chewed, as he lined up the sugar bowl, individual creamers, and then stacked them one by one, over and over.

Emily slid the coloring book and crayons in front of her before Trevor decided to eat the crayons.

Brad leaned on the table. "Em, Crystal and I have not reconciled, we're not renewing our vows. I don't know why she would have told you that. Actually, that's not true. I do know why." His eyes suddenly fixed with a sadness resembling hers.

Her stomach twisted up in knots, she hoped he ached too. She reached across the table and touched his hand. Her hand trembled and she yanked it back.

"You know, I made a mistake and I kick myself every day. I should have settled things with her when she left but instead, I did nothing. And you know what it got me? Her word against mine and frankly right now, she has me by the balls." Brad leaned back and tapped his hand on the table. The waitress arrived with their coffee and Trevor's juice.

"Thank you."

She only nodded as she walked away.

Brad ripped off the paper surrounding the straw and

dunked it in Trevor's apple juice.

Emily studied the man. What was he talking about?

His face flushed. "Sorry, Em, I didn't mean to be so graphic." He waved his hand for her to forget it and slurped his coffee. "You don't need this crap; you have your own struggles. I feel pretty low about how you got dragged into the middle of this shit, her shit, and how she treated you and Katy."

Her ears were ringing and the room didn't quite look right. She sucked in a deep breath, and then another. She opened her mouth to speak, but she couldn't think of anything to say. So she closed her mouth. He then reached for her hand as something similar to worry transformed those hard brown eyes.

Emily snatched her hand back. "Brad, you need to stop. I don't understand. What the hell are you talking about? How does she have you by the balls? What's going on? No more games, I swear to God, I feel as if you two crammed me into a shooting gallery at a carnival and I'm the target."

Gobs of blue dripped out of Trevor's mouth. He'd found a crayon and was chewing the paper off now along with bits of the crayon. Emily reached across the table. "Trevor, no, spit it out."

Brad jammed his fingers in Trevor's mouth and pulled out what was left of the blue crayon, and then used a napkin to wipe his face. Emily made sure, this time, she'd confiscated all the crayons. Trevor whined and reached for the crayons, which of course, he wanted back. "Brad, more crackers." Emily wiped the bits of crayon and spit off the table, and Brad dumped a pile of crackers in front of Trevor. "Here give me that." Emily took the soiled napkins and dumped them in the garbage by the door.

She felt grounded when she slid back in her seat. Trevor ate his crackers and swung his legs knocking the bottom of the booth, thud, thud. They'd better hurry. His crackers were almost gone.

Brad tapped his hand on the back of the booth. His face colored. "I never should have let her back in. That was my mistake and since I never filed for legal separation or abandonment of Trevor—full custody..." He threw his hands in the air and leaned back. "Let's just say, she's one smart B…" He almost said it but caught himself before the vulgar word slipped.

He glanced over at the waitress who raised her eyebrows from where she lingered behind the cappuccino machine. "She's seen a lawyer and had a plan before she walked back into my house. She knew exactly what to say and do. I screwed up. And I can't force her to leave. I'm the one that has to leave if I want a separation. And I can't take Trevor. She said I threatened and abused her and threw her out after Trevor was born. And that she suffered from depression, didn't know her rights. And now she's back because of Trevor having autism, she's threatened to take him, because this therapy is abusive. She believes because he was born this way, he is to live this way. He needs to be respected for who he is. She's even gone so far to put him on a waiting list for an institution in California, specializing in autistic children. She's using Trevor; for what reason, I don't know yet. But I can't, no I won't let her do that to my little boy." His eyes filled with tears as he placed his hand protectively on top of Trevor's head.

Emily wanted to leap up, race out to the ranch and give the woman a tongue lashing. "What do you mean she's threatened to take Trevor? She can't handle him. An institution, what the hell … she can't do that!" Emily slammed both hands on the table.

Brad grabbed her arms, jerked her forward. The man and woman across the room watched and whispered behind their hands. "Calm down, Em. I won't let her get away with it."

Emily lowered her voice, shooting a meaningful glance at Trevor. "I'm sorry, Brad but what the hell does she think she's doing? She hasn't spent any time with him. She avoids him. Her body language alone screams out how uncomfortable she is around him. She doesn't know him, she can't stand to be in the same room with him and he picks up on that."

"She can't fake motherly concern. He won't respond to her. She freaks him out. I don't understand why anyone would stoop that low. She's his mother; doesn't she want what's best for him?" Emily couldn't hold back the venom, she tried, she really did. She'd always tried to give everyone the benefit of the doubt, hadn't she? But this was too much. Trevor wasn't hers. But she wanted him to be.

"Em, you're right, but I need to think of Trevor. I already got raked over the coals by my lawyer. I need to listen to him. Follow what he says to win this and get her out of my life."

Understanding what really happened didn't make the hurt any less. How long had the woman planned to drive a wedge between her and Brad? It was odd if you thought about it. Her timing in coming home, just when her and Brad had developed a closeness. They'd almost consummated their relationship. She winced, as her mind dreamed up "what ifs" and "what might have been". "Brad, I'm so sorry, I should have known better. Please, if there's anything I can do?"

Brad clammed up and looked away. He reached for his wallet, threw a ten on the table.

"Are you finished?"

"Yes." Emily snatched her groceries and slid out. Brad followed with Trevor. The sun dipped lower, but was still nice and warm. Emily stopped and faced Brad. "Thanks for the coffee and for buying my groceries." She didn't want to walk away. She hated these awkward moments, and smiled one of those tense awkward smiles. Emily squatted in front of Trevor. "Bye, Trevor." He stared at the ground. He made no notice of her. Did he know she was even there? "He's regressed." Emily stood and didn't miss the way Brad flinched. "You know Brad; I've stayed silent about a lot of things. But Trevor deserves better than to be victimized because of a greedy, selfish mother. Look at him."

Brad flushed and touched the top of Trevor's head. "I know, Em, but I promise you, I'll start his therapy again. I know you're right. She's fighting me right now."

"She's wrong, Brad." Tears misted, blurring Brad. "To not help any child, to deny them therapy is cruel. Would you deny a child with cancer, his treatment?"

"That's not the same, Em. A child with cancer is fighting for their life."

She wanted to hit him. "What kind of life will Trevor have if he can't function?" Brad squeezed her shoulder. His eyes turned kinder.

"Hey, hey, Em, I know what you're saying. And I love your passion. You showed me remember? And you did everything you could to help Trevor. And I promise you I'll win. Remember your words, 'don't give up'."

He was still touching her. And that touch was doing all kinds of weird things to her resolve. He was under her skin. He managed to make every part of her hot and cold, anxious, happy, and wanting to leap up to the moon. After the hurt and pain he caused her, why did he still affect her so? "I should go." He dropped his hand, but neither turned away. So finally, Emily looked down, shifted her grocery bag to the other hand and backed away.

"Em." He called out. "Are you walking?"

"It's only a few blocks." Emily waved her hand and backed away.

"Jump in; I'll give you a ride." Brad gestured to his dark blue one ton.

He stepped toward her, one step, two steps. He wasn't giving her a choice. "All right."

Brad shoved Trevor's booster to the middle and buckled him in. He placed Emily's groceries in the back of the truck. Emily climbed in beside Trevor, Brad closed her door and strode around the front of the truck, waving to a couple walking who smiled and waved back. Brad climbed in and said nothing as he placed his arm along the back of the seat; his fingers brushed Emily's shoulder as he backed up. The touch lingered, distracted so she didn't realize Brad hadn't asked where she lived. In fact, he knew where to turn. "How'd you know where I live?" She pointed out the window and Brad pulled in front of her house.

He shut off the truck; winked when he finally faced her. "I asked around. Not many places to rent, Em. You were easy to find."

Her mouth opened to say something. But she couldn't put two sensible words together. She glanced out her window and laughed, until tears glistened. She touched Trevor's arm beside her, he watched her for the first time today. "Can you come in for a while?" Trevor kicked his legs back and forth; he was reaching for her now. "Please." He glanced out his window.

"Sure."

Thrilled, she wanted to bounce up and down on her seat and clap her hands like a little kid. But she didn't. And she didn't try to hide the easy smile that lifted her up. However, she shoved that cynical protective voice that piped up, *bad idea*, away in that locked cubby where she'd shoved her self-esteem and self-worth for so many years. Damn it all to hell, she wanted this time with him. And she'd take every minute she could get.

Emily unbuckled Trevor and Brad grabbed Emily's groceries. She led the way into her tiny neat bungalow. She wiggled the lock that frequently stuck with her key. She shoved open the door that often jammed on warmer days. "Em, call your landlord; get him to fix this door. Put in a new lock." Brad studied the doors seal, running his hand up and over the inside doorframe. Maybe some women would find that annoying, but Emily didn't. It'd be nice to have a man to handle those details.

Emily led Trevor to the toy box in the corner of the small cozy living room. It was by no means a bright house;

it was one of the older box style houses from the fifties. Emily pulled out Katy's Barbie cars, blocks and grabbed her doily from the table. Trevor didn't need to be told what to do. He plopped down on his side driving the cars in front of his face, back and forth.

Brad was gone when Emily stood up. She wandered into the small square kitchen. Brad had unloaded her groceries onto the round hardwood table, surrounded by four small pine chairs. Brad faced Emily and held up the bag of ripple chips and gestured toward the dip, Cheezies, a can of ginger ale and carton of milk. He raised his eyebrows. "Planning a party, Em?"

"Ha, ha," Emily stepped in and grabbed the bag of chips and stuffed it in the cupboard by the fridge, along with the rest of the junk food. "I was planning on treating myself—dinner and a movie."

He frowned and looked around. "Where's Katy?"

Smiling, she put the milk in the fridge. "Bob has her for the weekend. His mom's in town."

Brad leaned on the counter beside her. There really wasn't a whole lot of room in the kitchen. Brad, all lean, solid, a tall gorgeous man, took up more than an average man's share of space. She moved around him, brushing his arm, his back. Sweet torture, Emily had to wonder if he deliberately continued to stand so close. She couldn't think and felt heat rush her cheeks. So she grabbed the kettle and filled it with water. "Excuse me, Brad." He slid over a step, so she needed to reach behind him to plug in the kettle. She couldn't think. "Tea?"

He shook his head, smiling in a most unsettling way. "No thanks. So how are things going with him?" He flicked his hand.

"Paperwork's done for legal separation and I've asked my lawyer to file for divorce as soon as it's signed. He's finally agreed to pay some child support." He blinked and then narrowed his eyes, his face taking on a darkness Emily had only seen a few times. "Are you telling me, he never paid you? I thought he was sending you something."

The truth was Emily hadn't told anyone. She'd been embarrassed by his childish behavior. "He sent a little bit at first. Then he'd forget."

"God dammit, Em, why didn't you say something? You need any help with him, you call me. I'll make sure he pays you." He moved away from the counter stalked toward Emily, and then leaned back against the counter.

She should have stopped herself. But it was too late by the time her reasoning brain kicked in. She slid her hand across his cheek, the stubble. His deep brooding eyes had her pausing and she pulled her fingers away as if she'd been burned.

Thankfully, the kettle whistled so she now had something to focus on. She yanked the plug from the outlet, grabbed the kettle and somehow sloshed out a heap of scalding water onto her hand. She dropped the kettle, steaming water pooled on the counter and covered her pink throbbing hand. "Shit."

She exhaled hard. Brad grabbed her hand and dragged her over to the sink, shoving her burned hand under the icy cold water. "Hold it here. Are you okay?"

Emily gritted her teeth and shook her head. "That was stupid. You must think I'm a klutz." She peered under lashes at the man who glanced at her in such a subtle way. What the hell was he thinking? She could never tell. He held his cards so close to his chest.

"No, I think you're a little nervous having me here."

When Emily tried to pull her hand away and out of the frigid water, Brad held tighter. "Leave it, you've got a bad burn. You got a towel?"

"In the bathroom." Emily glanced out the small single pane window above the sink. The sting decreased as her hand numbed. She could hear his heavy walk across the creaking floorboards on his way down the narrow hall to the only bathroom. She hoped he didn't notice the bare, dingy walls. She'd not unpacked yet, let alone hung pictures. This place was merely a stopgap to her permanent home. The tiny backyard was crammed with Katy's climber and an old swing set inherited with the property. The old wood fence was missing boards here and there and needed painting.

"How is it?" She didn't hear him come back.

"Doesn't hurt as long as I keep it in the icy water." She turned off the tap.

Brad handed her a small peach towel. "Sit down." He pulled out one of the wooden chairs. Brad dragged out another chair, stretching out his long legs in front of him when he sat. "How about some coffee? I can make you some?" He burst out laughing.

"I think in order to save your other hand, let's skip the coffee. I need to get Trevor home for dinner anyway." Brad glanced around the corner. Emily could hear Trevor rustling in the toy box.

"Stay for dinner, please." He tilted his head and allowed a cat like grin to lighten his face. "That'd be nice, I've missed your cooking. I'm sure Trevor would appreciate a home cooked meal."

Emily didn't wait. She jumped up and yanked open the fridge, pulling out a package of ground beef. She fried the hamburger, adding seasoning, and sauce, boiled potatoes and threw together a casserole. She tossed together a salad while Brad chatted and lingered beside her.

Even through dinner, the conversation remained light and carefree, and she didn't miss the appreciation he groaned after his first bite. Trevor was restless. He ate some with his fingers, and then slipped away leaving his fork sticking out of his mashed potatoes, back to the toys. When they finished eating, Emily washed and Brad dried. He searched her cupboards as he put the dishes away. "I've missed you, Em."

She dropped the dishrag in the soapy water, and met his reflection in the darkened window in front of her. The illusion he cast toward her was one filled with yearning and regret. She turned around, her heart hammered in her chest. She couldn't catch her breath. She glanced at the clock on the wall. She didn't want him to leave. Her mind raced, doing everything it could, short of pulling a rabbit out of her hat, to find a way to keep him here. "Let's go sit in the living room. Unless you want coffee?"

"No, I'm good."

Emily wandered behind Brad. Her eyes dropped to ogle his swagger and the fine way he filled out his jeans. She loved the way he walked, and she remembered all too well how tight his ass was the one time they'd almost… Emily nearly choked when she realized what she was doing. And Brad watched her in way she was positive, he knew where her thoughts had gone. She cleared her throat and darted to the TV. "Let me put a movie in for Trevor." She threw in *Peter Pan*, turning down the volume. Trevor jumped on the faded leather sofa, the one that had seen better days. Brad sank into the matching loveseat angled beside the sofa. Emily darted a glance at the cozy spot beside Brad, but curled in beside Trevor. She wrapped the purple afghan over Trevor's legs when he rested his head on the pillow.

"It was a great meal Em. I've been cooking for me and Trevor and I'm probably the worst cook around. Mary comes only two days a week, she won't stay long. I've asked her to come more, but she refused, said those two days take everything out of her having to deal diplomatically with Crystal."

Emily watched him. She missed the time they'd shared at night, talking.

"So who looks after Trevor when you work, Brad? I mean you have a ranch to run."

"I take him with me. Needless to say I don't get much done."

She didn't realize she was holding her breath, until it escaped in a whoosh.

"You can't honestly believe I would leave Trevor with

her, do you?"

Emily flushed. She reached out to touch him, but he pulled away. "Brad, I'm sorry. I didn't know what to think. Everything that happened … when you allowed her to stay… How could I not? I don't think you know how much I care about you. When she showed up, you turned your back on me, on us. I didn't know what to think."

He shook his head and leaned forward; brushed away the tear that traced it's way down her cheek. "No, Em, I'm sorry, I let you think the worst of me. I was trying to protect you. I didn't want to drag you into the mess I created."

He pressed his back into the loveseat, running his fingers through his hair.

"I screwed up, Em, big time. I should have filed the minute she walked out the door. Instead, that is the one area of my life I allowed to slide. If that were a business, I would have protected myself. Instead, I kept putting it off and now look. The other night she actually had the nerve to suggest we have another baby in the same breath she brought up the institution for Trevor. Trying to justify they could help him. It was as if she wanted him replaced, out of sight, out of mind. I've started paying real close attention. She leaves the room whenever Trevor's there and goes out of her way to not spend any time with him. She has this iron wall around her heart and won't let him in." He moved closer and intertwined his fingers with Emily. "It's not that she's not capable of loving him, but I realized what it is. She's scared. She's not strong like you. She's closed herself off to protect herself."

"So what are you going to do?" Emily asked with a slight catch in her breath.

"I've filed for divorce, if she fights me for the ranch, so be it. It's been in my family for two generations. But this is about Trevor. I'll fight her for him. She's already threatened to take Trevor if I try to leave, but my lawyer says I've got a real good chance. Especially since she's already left once." He let out a heavy sigh and then glanced over at the clock in the darkened room. Well past nine, and Trevor had fallen asleep beside Emily.

He stood up. She knew he was going to leave. "Don't go. Trevor can sleep in Katy's bed. Please." What was he thinking? He studied her in an odd way before framing her cheeks with the palm of his hands. He then slowly lowered his mouth to hers, tenderly at first, brushing her lips with a light and teasing air, and then something snapped in him as he pulled her up. It was by no means anything gentle, a fierce possession letting her know what she'd hoped would happen tonight, would.

Chapter Thirty-One

Brad broke away; he rocked her heart. The soft play of Disney music filled the background. Brad scooped Trevor off the sofa and set him in Katy's bed. Emily covered him with the pink comforter and stepped into the hall with Brad. The way he watched Trevor, she realized this man would move mountains for his son.

When he turned to her, she reached out to him. But her hand trembled, when she wondered if she was what Brad really wanted. He must have sensed her hesitation, as he leaned down and whispered to her the words she needed to hear.

"It's all right. It's just you and me in this moment, Em." He lowered his head and his lips touched hers. His passion was unrestrained; a kiss hard, deep, one that told a woman she meant something. He lifted her in his arms, breaking the kiss only to ask, "The bedroom in here?"

"Uh, huh."

Her heart thudded as he set her on the bed, pressing his body into her, once again capturing her mouth with his. It was amazing how this man, and his overwhelming power, could tell her with a touch, a caress, that she was wanted—she was needed She ached for him, he too seemed hurried as he broke away, unbuttoning her blouse and her jeans and had her naked beneath him. He yanked off his shirt and pants, tossing everything in a heap on the floor. The hall light teased the room with a hint of light, enough that Emily swallowed hard at the image of this man. *Oh wow, he's magnificent.* With clothes on, he looked great. Seeing him now in all his naked splendor, took her breath away. He had a solid mass of muscles on his wide expanse of chest. Slim hips, no beer belly on this man, his lean hard stomach, the shape and strength of his thighs were solid and artfully constructed. There was no indecision, just anticipation and awareness that this man knew how to make love to a woman.

He moved with her. She twined her legs with his; he gazed deeply into her eyes for a few seconds, before leaning down and paying homage to her small perky breasts. His tongue touched and licked the first nipple, then he slowly took it in his mouth, lavishing, while being attentive to the other, to all of her. His hand drifted down, touching, caressing. Sweet torment was building, as she rustled against him when a tremble unearthed her.

Tossing her head back and forth, she didn't know how much more she could take and she finally pleaded with him, "Brad … please, now."

"Not yet, we have time; tonight I'm going feel you buck beneath me, over and over." His hand continued to explore up the line of her thighs, pressing as he spread her legs wide. He explored and teased, lightly tracing the soft jewel where her legs joined, feeling how wet and ready she was for him. She couldn't hold still as he slipped his finger in. He was enjoying her torment while she begged him to complete her.

Emily grasped his shoulders. She tried to pull him to her, but he wouldn't move, instead he watched and held her burning gaze. It was maddening how he toyed with her bringing her to the brink of madness. She moaned, unable to suppress it any longer. He covered her mouth with his, a kiss so powerful and deep, his tongue mimicking the age-old art of loving. He spread her legs wide, guiding her to wrap them around his waist, running his hands smoothly over her curves. Cupping her buttocks, he slowly entered her. The way he watched her, she knew she was completely at his mercy. He touched her lip with the tip of his tongue; peered at her through hooded eyes. She gave herself up completely. A full surrender that left her gasping, flying and soaring together to music all their own. Something cracked the thin wall around her heart and she shut her eyes, swallowed in the age-old dance they shared together and allowed herself to let go. When she opened her eyes, he was watching her with a catlike grin, as he lay sprawled on top of her, pressing her into the mattress. She didn't want him to move; she wanted to absorb the magnitude of the feelings he'd managed to elicit from each cell, deep inside. A paradise she didn't want to end. Never in her life had she experienced this intense passion. A man, who knew what he wanted, understood what she needed and how to make her lose control.

He leaned on his elbows, looking down at her and smoothed back her hair. She saw the fire glitter in his eyes still smoking within her. He pulled away, rolled on his back and threw his arm over his forehead. *Did he regret what we did?* Her heart sank for just a minute. She leaned over and touched his chest ever so lightly, almost fearful he may flee at any given moment. "Are you okay?"

He cupped her cheek, and she kissed his palm absorbing his touch. He winced as he pulled her close. Surrounding her with his arms, her legs tangled with his; he brushed his lips across her forehead and traced circles down her back.

She could feel something change inside him, as if he were pulling away. She waited with her cheek resting against his chest. She sucked in her bottom lip and pressed her teeth into the tender flesh, waiting for reality to speak. For him to say the words *Yeah, Em thanks, this was great, but I got to get Trevor home.*

He smacked his lips. He sucked in a breath. Okay, here it comes. She scrunched her eyes closed. "Em, are you on the pill? I mean, we didn't use a condom, which was really stupid." She darted up and looked him squarely in the eye while his hands ran up her back, down and over her bottom. She blinked, trying to understand what he said. He raised one brow, expecting an answer. She blinked again.

"No … there was never a need, I haven't well, had … well, let's just say it's been over a year, but it's the wrong time of the month. I'm pretty good at knowing when it's … you know…" This was really embarrassing, even after what they shared. She'd never thought about it.

His lips twitched at her demure way of explaining. Then he held her face between the palms of his hands, forcing her to look at him and he crooked his eyebrow up. "Em, come on just admit it, we didn't use any protection, and there's a pretty big chance you're carrying my kid now."

She shivered, at the thought of carrying his child. Wow, until now, she'd not thought of having more "God, how I'd love to have your baby." Where had they come from? She slapped her hand over her mouth, wishing it back. It was too soon; she could scare him away. But she was so tired of hiding her feelings. She didn't want to take it back.

Brad said nothing; just watched her in an odd distant way. She wanted to ask if he wanted more children, if he'd stay. She wanted to know what he was thinking. But she said nothing as she slid her leg with his and snuggled in closer. And for a moment as she shut her eyes, dreamed of a forever connection.

Chapter Thirty-Two

Emily rested her elbow on the kitchen table. She sipped on a second cup of coffee, searching the hot black liquid for some sign or answer. The wall clock ticked, after eleven, Bob promised to return Katy before lunch on Sunday, so he could pull in anytime.

Brad had stayed all night. And true to his word, he'd made love to her throughout the night, waking her several times. Although tired, she felt more energized than she had in years. She'd cooked a big breakfast for Brad and Trevor. They'd lingered over a few cups of coffee. Neither wanted this to end. But he had no choice. He had a ranch to run. He needed to leave.

Never had Emily felt the intense comfort of being with the right guy; the one who sends your heart and soul to the natural high and if they leave, you'd swear your heart will blister into a million pieces. Emily held up her bare ring finger, not even a flicker of remorse because with Bob, she'd never experienced this kind of passion, this kind of bliss. Waking in Brad's arms, as he slowly entered her was a passion far more vivid, more potent, she'd swear she'd died and gone to heaven, or someplace close. Even the shower they shared after the sun had come up had been filled with such creative passion. Emily rinsed out her mug and wandered to the front window. She sighed, wishing Brad to return. But he left after kissing her long and thoughtfully, without promises, or frilly words—nothing. He had a dragon to slay, a conflict to end. Afterward he'd return and be her everything.

Chapter Thirty-Three

For the first time in what felt like forever, Brad felt the oppressive weight lift off. Watching Emily come apart beneath him, her shy glances and her tender touch, it was the purest, simplest form of love. He shook his head. Five years ago, he'd never have given her a second look. But right now, he wanted to get down on his knees and thank whomever steered her his way. Emily was a complicated, wise and powerful soul and Brad knew the short, feisty, brown haired beauty would fight heaven and earth for what was right. The opposite of the shallow flashy women he'd always gravitated to.

Brad turned down his long dirt driveway, and felt the heaviness drop back down on him like a sack of potatoes. How could he hate a place he loved so much?

He swallowed hard as he remembered what a shallow, stupid ass he was. He created this mess because of who he was. He loved that superficial lust with Crystal, she looked good hanging off his arm and that's all he ever wanted, anything deeper would have sent him running for the hills.

Brad scratched his head and glanced at Trevor as he remembered Crystal's horror, the day she found out she was pregnant. Brad had laughed and brushed it off to simple hysterics, that she was scared of being a mother and convinced himself she'd get used to it. Only as he allowed himself to face the truth, did he now realize it was more than that; Crystal never wanted children, because she was still very much a child.

She couldn't care for someone who depended on her. She wasn't that strong, or was she too selfish? Reflecting and admitting the truth was a bitter pill to swallow; he cared for her then. A one-sided deal.

Crystal looked after the surface stuff, spending his money, redecorating the house, enjoying a lifestyle she actually believed she was entitled to.

An only child doted upon by her mother and father. They were by no means wealthy, but they'd given her anything and everything she'd ever wanted. There were no teachings of the value of money, commitment and responsibility. But then, Brad hadn't listened either.

His daddy was a good man. He'd pulled him aside weeks before the wedding, reminding him this was his choice and his alone to live with. That he would never say another word, but he expected him to listen now. Girls like Crystal were fun to play with. She was shallow and not the marrying kind; she'll never be devoted to you and any kids you want. Brad had been furious and lashed out at his father. He'd told him he was just jealous he'd found someone this dazzling. His father nearly hit him. Brad winced now as he squeezed the steering wheel in his truck. He was ashamed; he wished his father would've decked him. He deserved it. Because Brad hadn't spoken to his father since, his mom, infrequent, but he never told her what was going on.

As the oldest, the ranch passed to Brad. His father and younger brother bought 10,000 acres down on the Yucatan Peninsula—their idea of a small ranch.

He visited his mother once, with Crystal right after Trevor was born. His father then was in Panama, whether planned or coincidence, Brad didn't know. Now he wished for his daddy's advice, to make peace and bridge the gulf widening with each day's passing.

When he and Crystal married he looked after her, handled everything. He paid the bills, was generous with providing her money and credit cards. She'd no concept of value and continually exceeded her credit limit.

The first time he spoke with her, he'd been blunt. "I'm not an untapped well."

She panicked and carried on in such a way anyone would have thought the world was coming to an end. He was astounded by what she spent on clothes alone. She never batted an eye at dropping a few thousand on a designer outfit. Shopping was her favorite past time and he'd always given in, especially after she became pregnant.

So when did the blinders come off?

After she had Trevor, Brad truly believed she'd take one look at him and fall in love, just as he had. That she'd stay home; become a good wife and doting mother. He was sure the inbred nurturing instinct that existed in women from the beginning of time would finally emerge. He just assumed it was natural.

But nothing went as planned. After she gave birth, she'd refused to hold him. He'd watched painfully as she seemed to go into a depressive slump, more concerned with how she looked and what giving birth and the pregnancy had done to her body.

Brad made excuses for her behavior. It was the ordeal of giving birth, she was tired and she'd come around. But the nurses new better, he'd ignored their knowing looks, especially after her outright refusal to breast-feed when the nurse had encouraged her to try and get him latched on. The nurse tried to explain the importance of a mother's milk. She'd screamed back she didn't want her breasts to get *saggy*.

Brad didn't worry too much as many mothers chose to bottle-feed. It really wasn't that big of a deal.

Things escalated after they were home. She wanted a nanny for Trevor. Brad put his foot down and refused. He lost his temper. "As Trevor's mother, I expect you look after him." She'd screamed like a two year old and called her mother. Of course, the next thing Brad knew, his mother-in law moved in and was looking after the baby. Betty had a heart condition. After weeks of looking after the baby and Crystal, dark circles appeared under her eyes. Brad sat her down. "What the hell are you doing, Betty?"

She cried and hung her head. "I'm so sorry, Brad, me and Crystal's daddy are to blame. We loved her so much and we struggled when we were growing up; we didn't want her to have to do without. Not like we did. I'm so sorry, Brad; we never taught her responsibility or how to make her own way. We made everything easy for her."

Brad felt horrible for the woman's pain, but he didn't make it easier. "She expects everything to be handed to her, for you to wait hand and foot on her. You have to stop. You're not helping the situation. She'll never grow up."

Betty had stiffened her lip. "She's my daughter and I love her. And I love that Grandbaby. I can't stop." And she didn't, she doted all her love on Trevor until a few months later, she suffered a stroke in her sleep one night and passed away in the hospital a few days later. It had nearly destroyed Crystal.

Crystal had been like a lost child, turning to Brad, not knowing what to do. Her father had died ten years earlier. Brad remained hopeful that now she'd finally become a mother to Trevor. Instead, what happened rocked his world. She packed her bags and slipped out of the house a week later, leaving Trevor alone. Mary Haske had arrived to clean just before lunchtime and heard the pitiful wail of a crying baby. Brad had foolishly left him with Crystal and he headed to the North field.

Mary had searched the house looking for Crystal. When Brad drove the tractor in to have lunch, he found a ruffled Mary, irate and panicked, holding Trevor in her arms.

She must have been watching, as she raced out of the house. Her eyes damp and red rimmed, and his heart dropped like lead into his stomach when he heard those gut-wrenching words. She'd found Trevor alone crying in his crib, no one there to hear him. She had been furious and demanded to know where Crystal was. His blood ran cold, at first he thought she was hurt somewhere, as he hurried into the house to search. Instead, he'd felt the center drop out of him when he raced into the bedroom, pulled open the closet to discover her clothes, makeup, jewelry, everything was gone. The fury that stole over him, that she could have left Trevor alone, made him physically shake with fear. What if Mary hadn't come? He'd collapsed to the floor right in front of Mary. Then when it sunk in, he put his fist through the wall and bloodied his knuckles. That physical pain was welcome. The other was not. The tears stung the back of his eyes as he held his boy tight for a long time, before leaving him in the care of Mary Haske.

Brad spent a week tracking Crystal down. It was through his credit cards he was able to find her in Hawaii, at a beachside resort. He'd left several messages with the hotel operator. But she never returned his calls. Two days later, Brad had been pole axed as he'd waited in her hotel room, when she came in wearing a string bikini, laughing, and giggling with some guy.

He still remembered the humiliation as he left without her. Crystal stayed away. The weeks turned into months. He kept track of where she was. She only phoned when she needed money and never once did she ask about Trevor.

Now after all these years she'd come home, to suddenly be Trevor's mother? He knew it wasn't true. She could barely stand being in the same room with him. And if by chance she was, she always found a reason to leave. Brad would never be that careless again. He saw it in her eyes; she worried Brad would demand her to look after him. No, he would never do that again. Then it struck him, it was the security he offered. He'd become her safety net. He handled everything for her, allowed her to have anything she wanted. Even with her gone for the last few years, he foolishly continued to pay for everything for her, but no more. She'd made a big mistake. She'd used this child, his precious child. And she'd forced the one woman who truly cared for him and Trevor, out of his house. Emily, who had fought for Trevor's future and helped him see what Trevor truly needed.

"Home sweet home, Trevor."

He'd barely lifted Trevor from the truck when Crystal stormed out, decked out, as if she was going to town, wearing black jeans, a white blouse, not a hair out of place.

And the way she dug in with each step, Brad knew hell would be a lot more peaceful.

He held Trevor and watched this pitiful, greedy woman and the anger she held close. How could he have loved, let alone worshipped the ground she walked on? There had to be something wrong with him.

"Just where the fuck were you? I waited up for you all night!" She balled her fists and planted them on her hips.

Brad put Trevor down. He could feel him tense as he started swaying and rocking back and forth, from one foot to the other. The squeaks were becoming more pronounced lately, to an "eek, eek" and "click, click" with his tongue. "Okay, Trevor, let's get you changed." Brad bent down and picked Trevor up and set him on his shoulders. He stepped around Crystal.

She dogged his heels like one of those irritating little Chihuahuas that don't know how to shut up. "You were with her weren't you? That slut." The accusation was laced with so much venom that Brad needed to restrain himself from turning and hitting her. Trevor reminded him by tugging his hair.

She bumped into him at the door, practically stepped on his foot. He darted around so fast he almost knocked her over with the force of his words, "Get the fuck away from me, you're scaring Trevor. I'll talk to you after I get him settled."

Smart lady, she didn't follow.

Brad plopped Trevor in front of the TV, and put in a Walt Disney movie. When he turned around, he saw her standing there just inside the door, impatiently tapping the toe of her designer boot. Brad moved at a speed that had Crystal's mouth hanging open. He grabbed her and dragged her with him into the kitchen, releasing her with such force she almost fell against the table.

He crossed his arms and surveyed the kitchen, the dirty dishes stacked in the sink, on the counter, Cliff and Mac had obviously come in to eat. He'd end that now. They had their own kitchen in the house in back. Until things were settled, they were going to have to make their own meals in their own place.

He dragged his eyes over her, and then dismissed her as he turned away. She planted herself in his face and tossed her long blond mane over her shoulder.

"Just where the hell were you? I demand some answers, as your wife I have a right…" Her face paled and she closed her mouth.

Brad raised his hands, now shaking; he squeezed his fists as he loomed over her. Maybe she realized how close he was to strangling her. "You have a right to what?" His words were low, deathly quiet, with a bite so sharp she took another step back. She swallowed and her eyes widened. She should be scared.

Brad stalked to the table dragged out a chair and pointed. "Sit down and keep your voice down, I'll not have you upsetting Trevor anymore."

She tossed her long hair over her shoulder and acted as if she was the injured party. She glared right back. But the slight tremor on her lower lip betrayed her. She hesitated a second, and then sat.

She gazed up and then flushed. Maybe she realized she'd pushed him too far. Even Brad worried he couldn't contain the wild animal that sought to break free.

She squirmed. He crossed his arms as his hair prickled the back of his neck with a warning not to turn his back on her. She was clever and spiteful and if he underestimated her, he was positive he would live to regret it.

"I want you to leave." How'd he get his voice so calm?

An indignant righteous flush stole over her face. She looked away and sat up straighter in her chair, tilting her head in a way that usually had him softening inside. He nearly laughed; blinking at, and thankful for, his new found awareness. Maybe she realized it, because he'd swear he could see the wheels turn in that sharp mind of hers.

"No, I will not leave and you can't make me." She studied her fingers, toyed with the large square diamond ring; he'd spent a small fortune to propose.

"My lawyer's filed the necessary papers for divorce. As for Trevor, I've requested sole custody and guardianship." He knew his mistake as soon as she jumped out her chair and clawed at his face.

He brushed her away.

"I will not leave and you're not getting custody of Trevor, I'm his mother and no court will take him away from me." She was like a rabid animal that wouldn't back down.

"You don't give a crap about Trevor; you spend no time with him. You never have. For God's sake Crystal, just go. I'll be generous with my settlement. You'll want for nothing."

She shook her head with such steely control. "No Brad, you're my husband and she can't have you."

So it wasn't just the money. The pieces of the puzzle were dropping into place. Hold your cards closer to your chest. She knows things she shouldn't. But how? He paced the kitchen, turning his back; a cold sweat broke out. When he turned back and glimpsed her cat like smirk, he knew. There was a traitor in this midst. He didn't know who, or did he? "Trevor will be starting his therapy again as soon as I can arrange it and you'll not interfere!" He took a few steps toward her. "My lawyer's drawn up the paper work for custody and the order for divorce. If you continue to fight me, you'll get nothing. I've been very generous in my settlement and offer for spousal support. This offer I'm making is one time only, so if I were you, I would do some serious thinking." Brad needed to leave now. He had work to do, not just at the ranch. But to overturn every rock and find out whom the traitor was. He bundled Trevor in his coat, and carried him out the door.

He put Trevor in the truck and drove to where the men were working, a downed fence at the west end of the property. He dragged his cell phone from his pocket and dialed the number programmed in his phone.

"Hello." The soft musical voice had always given him hope.

"Hi Mom, is Dad there? I really need to talk to him."

Chapter Thirty-Four

Monday morning brought sunshine in the warm spring air. Walking into work, she was still wistful from her time with Brad. She must have jumped a mile when her boss strode up behind her.

"I need to have a word with you Emily, can you come to my office." His tone was chilly.

It was then she noticed Suzanne one of the other workers behind the till, appeared awkward and averted her eyes. Emily followed Jake into his office. "Shut the door please."

Her hands trembled and it felt like jumping jacks bounced around in her stomach. She wracked her brain. Did she do something wrong? Jake sat on the other side of the desk, his tightly clasped hands folded in front of him. "I'm going to have to let you go."

The floor fell out from under her. If he had sucker punched her, it would have hurt less. A confusing haze spun around her, as she sucked in a deep shaky breath, maybe she didn't hear him right. She stared into his closed off eyes. Then he visibly colored as he awkwardly leaned back in his chair, glancing down at his hands before meeting Emily's gaze. This didn't make any sense, just last week he called her into his office, praising her for what a great job she was doing. He'd even given her a two dollar an hour raise, *what could have happened between then and now?* She couldn't for the life of her figure out what she'd done wrong.

"I … I don't understand," She somehow managed to get the words out, asking, but feeling gutted; her face flushed with hurt and humiliation.

Jake was now having a hard time looking at her. When he finally did, he gritted his teeth before looking over at her with a sympathetic appeal in his eyes. "I'll give you a great reference, but I'm in a bind." He splayed his fingers in front of him. "I had a call from one of my largest accounts and they threatened to pull it unless I let you go. It was some problem they had with you." He shook his head and raised his defensive voice when Emily tried to appeal. "I'm just a small operation and if they pull it, I won't be in business anymore."

Emily was struck dumb as to who would want to do this to her. Leaning forward, furious at the injustice, she was determined to have all her questions answered. "Who was it that wanted me fired?" There was no way she was going anywhere until she found out and personally addressed it. It had to be a misunderstanding.

Looking away, he closed his eyes. "Emily, please. I don't want any trouble and I'd rather not say. I don't want to be dragged into the middle of this."

"No, dammit it's not okay, I demand to know. No, I think I have a right to know and if you won't tell me, I'll contact the labor board or a lawyer if I have to and drag your ass through court for wrongful dismissal." She knew she'd gone too far with that last one, but she couldn't hold it back. She was being screwed over.

"Okay you want to know, I'll tell you, it was Brad Friessen and there's no way I can afford to piss off a guy like that." Standing up he was furious as he pointed to the door. "Now get out." Trembling with anger, he held out her check and waited impatiently for her to take it. Emily shook as she reached for the check, struggled for breath and tried to still the ringing in her ears. The implication of such a betrayal weighed heavily, *how could he?* She struggled to hold it together as she walked out past the customers, Suzanne and she prayed no one else she knew. She fought to suppress the tears as she hurried back to her rental house. The whole time her mind swam with images of

Brad. The questions, the pain, how this man, in less than forty-eight hours, had gone from making passionate unprotected love to her, to this. It just didn't make sense. She cursed everything she could upon him, and then upon all men. She wanted to hate him. Only it didn't feel right after everything they'd shared. His confession, what Crystal had done. That was not a man who didn't care. One who would then turn around and try to gut her entire existence. No, the Brad she knew would never have done anything that despicable. Her head was driving her crazy with that voice playing devil's advocate. He'd let her leave his home, but he'd explained that. Then there were the problems with Crystal, after all he'd let her stay. But then she was his wife. Even if she disappeared and abandoned her child, she'd no interest in being a mother to Trevor. She dropped her head in her hands as she raged, trying to make sense of what happened. It was beginning to drive her crazy. He confided in her about why Crystal was still there and legally his hands were tied. Or had he just said that, for her benefit? She wanted to scream, she was so confused, none of this made any sense as she stormed up the walkway to the small house she rented. Unlocking the door, she went in and closed it tightly behind her. Tossing her purse down on the leather couch, she sank down beside it. The burgundy cloth covering the easy chair was so worn it was beginning to fray along the seams. Slowly scanning the room with her eyes, the toys were scattered by the green plastic tub. The crayons and coloring book littered the chipped, wooden coffee table.

She leaned back, feeling gutted, her breath shaky. She couldn't fight the tears and didn't try. She was a messy crier and let the keening go. "Can things get any worse." Her thoughts wandered to Katy, and what they were to do.

She took a deep breath trying to still the hiccup and crying jag. She grabbed the box of Kleenex and blew her nose. Talking to anyone, they'd know she either had a cold or was crying. She just sat there and listened to the sound of the clock tick away. Then she knew what she needed to do. Her motions were almost robotic as walked to the door, and then froze when her hand touched the knob. She backed away, strode into the kitchen and grabbed the telephone. Before she allowed herself to think about what she was doing, she dialed the number. It rang just once before it was picked up and answered by that sugary sweet voice. Emily felt her stomach sink. *Hang up.* She heard it but she didn't listen. "I would like to speak to Brad, please."

There was a long pause on the other end, before she coolly asked, "Who's calling please?"

Bitch, she thought to herself, *she knows damn well whose calling.* "It's Emily. I'd like to speak with Brad please, now."

"My husband's not available at the moment. He's downtown picking up our tickets. We're getting ready to leave on a holiday together. It's kind of celebration. I'll tell him you called."

There it was another knife in her back. *What the hell was he doing, had he really just slept with her all night, with his son in the next room, and then gone home to her and reconciled.* A vacation, are you kidding? She looked at the phone and her heart sank, she couldn't believe he'd do this to her again. "Could you ask him to call me, it's important." She tried to keep the shake from her voice, but she failed miserably. Before she fell apart completely, she ended the call.

Laying her head down on the counter, she closed her eyes as she was unable to stop the sobs welling up inside. It felt like a vice had suddenly been squeezed around her chest and she allowed the pain to escape. Her knees gave out and she sank to the floor, letting go of everything she'd held together for so long. She cried, praying the pain swelling in her heart, threatening, in that moment to destroy her, would disappear. All the while cursing herself for being so stupid to allow this man to do this to her, again. As she sat there on the floor, long after her tears had dried up, she felt empty, like she had been pitched headfirst into an emotionless void. And it was then that it hit her, how she'd given herself so freely to him, opening herself up to this man—to Brad, in a way she'd never done before.

Chapter Thirty-Five

His father was Rodney Friessen. He was established, hard headed and respected. To reach out and call him was, for Brad, admitting he'd been wrong. But he was—wrong, that is. In the end, he swallowed his pride and sought the help he and Trevor needed. It had been a bitter pill to swallow. His Mom had picked up the extension after listening on the sidelines for half an hour. To his daddy's credit he never once said, "I told you so" or "you should have listened to me". Instead, he listened without judgment, and then offered his help and some solid advice for a viable plan to resolve this situation, which meant removing Trevor from this acidic environment. Telling his parents Trevor had autism had been heart wrenching. His mother cried but his father remained silent. Then they both said they would be on the next plane back to Seattle.

Two days later Brad picked up his parents from the floatplane he'd chartered from Seattle. They'd not seen Trevor since he was a baby, so he was unprepared for their welcome.

"Brad, where's my grandson." His mom, Becky, was short, gray haired, plump and flowing with life. She hugged him and then bent down to Trevor who stood hiding behind Brad's leg. She took his hand and talked to him. She pulled a wrapped present from her handbag, which he grabbed. His "eeks" and squeaks were quiet for the first time, as he unwrapped two hot wheels cars and an Elmo talking book.

"Cool gifts, Mom." Trevor seemed to think so too, as he sat on the grass and played with the first car he unwrapped.

His father was a tall man with short-cropped gray hair and deeply etched lines on his face. He hovered behind his wife, hesitant, the awkwardness still there. It wasn't until Brad extended his hand that his father reached out and pulled him into his arms instead. Their conversation was stilted at first, until his daddy pulled him aside to let him know they were prepared to stay as long as it took.

The plan was for Trevor to return with his grandparents, to Baja. He would stay with them until Brad resolved this battle with Crystal.

On the drive back to the ranch, his Mom told him of a lady she hired who had experience with autistic children. From the minute Becky got off the telephone with Brad, she'd researched autism, the therapy Brad told her about and how best they could help Trevor. She was glued to Trevor the entire ride back and insisted on walking the ranch before taking Trevor in.

When Crystal saw his parents arrive, she stumbled on the porch.

Becky cooked dinner. The conversation around the table flowed from the cattle, the dairy contract, and then to Trevor. His father was masterful, charming, when he wanted to be, and ruthless. But it was his Becky who suggested Trevor come and visit. Crystal was hesitant, but his father cornered her with his charisma, leaving her no room to maneuver. Right after dinner, Rodney produced a letter of consent. Brad signed it first, and then passed it to Crystal. He noted her reluctance as she glanced at the phone. But Becky soothed her ruffled feathers and had her sign before she could find an excuse and change her mind.

Brad's parents left in the morning, with the signed consent for customs and their grandson, Trevor.

"You call me as soon as you get things squared. Your Mom's right on top of what needs to be done for Trevor. So you focus on what you need to do."

"Thanks again, Daddy. And I'm sorry, I should have

listened."

"It's done, but you call me if you need help."

To have that support was like a return to the fold. For the first time, he felt his father had his back.

The fight with Crystal escalated the moment he returned home.

"You railroaded me, you and your parents. I never should have signed that letter."

Brad smiled as he walked out the door.

****

Brad was finishing a ham and cheese sandwich when Crystal strode in, dropping her leather coat on the chair and dumping her purse on the table. She kissed his cheek. "Surprise." She dropped two tickets on the table.

"What's this?" He picked them up and opened the flap.

"The Cook Islands, I booked us a beachside resort for ten days, nothing but sunshine, beach and being pampered, you and me. She traced her long painted nails up his arm.

"You're unbelievable." He pushed away his plate, threw down the tickets and walked out.

He was determined to do this right and heed his lawyers' advice to walk away from a fight. It was hard, especially the way she goaded him. He phoned Keith again and yelled. "Hurry and get me that court date. I want her out of my house."

Brad cancelled her credit cards, emptied their joint bank account before removing his name from the account. It was now solely hers. And he left firm instructions with the manager of the Bank; she no longer had access to any of his funds.

She'd stormed into the house when he was in his office. She'd thrown her purse at him, then a book and anything else she could grab. "You asshole, I was in the city shopping for a new pair of shoes and my card was declined. Do you have any idea how embarrassing that is, I tried every card and each one was declined. The manager was called and she took my cards and cut them up."

Brad leaned his head back and howled. He laughed so hard tears leaked out. "I'd have paid good money to see that, baby."

Of course, she grabbed his jade bookend and launched it at his head, he ducked thank goodness, and the glass unit behind him shattered.

Of course, the very next day Brad's lawyer received a very angry call from her lawyer. A demand for maintenance for his client or they'd be suing him for damages. It was going to get nasty.

"Brad, listen to me, she's already alleged in her suit against you she's seeking full custody of Trevor. But now according to her lawyer, she'll rescind this if you agree to drop the suit to divorce her, and reinstate her credit cards, and full access to your bank account."

"Keith, she's dreaming. I'm done with her; I'm not giving her nothing." Brad squeezed his cell phone as he stomped out of the barn.

"Let me finish. It gets better. According to her lawyer, Crystal's alleging undue cruelty to Trevor through this ABA therapy treatment you started. It seems they're able to track down some experts who'll cite recent claims that it leaves these children not only robotic, but also scarred with devastating long-term effects, like a syndrome similar to what veterans from the war suffer."

"I'm going in the house right now and I'm throwing her out. Trevor's with my parents. Let her fight me from somewhere else."

Keith shouted so loud Brad lifted the phone away from his ear. "I told you before to cool your temper. You do a stupid ass move like that and I guarantee you'll spend the night cooling your ass in a holding cell. And I'll leave you there. Then she'll have a restraining order against you by morning before you get out of lockup. The locks will be changed on your house and she'll have a fast track to gaining full custody of Trevor." When he hung up, ice water could have flowed through his veins. He shoveled out a few horse stalls before he'd calmed down, and then he called Keith back. "Listen Keith, you mentioned something about some experts who said this therapy for Trevor causes some war vet syndrome."

Keith let out a heavy sigh. "Brad, there was a court battle in Canada a few years back. A group of parents took the government to court to obtain medically necessary treatment for their autistic children. The court battle went to the Supreme Court of Canada. In the Auton case, The Supreme Court in BC dismissed the information Crystal's using from these experts as not valid, yet it was still published. Your Lovaas ABA therapy has been proven genuine, so we'll use her theory against her. But the judge may be swayed by her interest as a mother torn, not wanting the therapy, by all the perilous misinformation that's out there."

"Listen up, Brad. I'm going to warn you again, because she knows what buttons to push to set you off. Control that temper of yours, be smart, think before you say anything and call me if you're not sure." That last remark had brought a slight smile to his lips. Keith knew him well, too well sometimes.

"Plan B, I've hired a private detective I used to work with in Seattle. I guarantee you he'll dig and find any deep dark secret and skeleton we can use on Crystal."

Brad kicked at a pile of manure. "Keith, something's been bothering me—Crystal coming back when she did and knowing things that were going on at the ranch she shouldn't have. I don't know, it's as if she's got someone on the inside feeding her information."

"I'll get Byrd, my guy in Seattle, to check it out."

Brad stared at the house he loved with such venom. "Thanks, Keith."

He pocketed his phone and grabbed a rake. "May as well clean out the rest of these stalls."

* * * *

Two weeks and three days had passed since he last touched Emily. He should have called before now. If nothing else, to tell her how much he cared.

Keith called and he raced into town. They spent hours strategizing. When Brad left, he was distracted, but he didn't miss the small brunette who gasped, ducked her head and attempted to walk around him. "Whoa, Em, what are you doing?" He reached out and grasped her arm. But she yanked it away and when she raised her head, he was rocked by the blazing fire that seeped from her eyes. "Em, are you okay? I know I should have called." Whoa, if the sparks flying from her were any indication, she was madder than a nest of angry hornets.

"Well, funny you should ask. Just answer one question for me. What kind of kicks do you get by pulling that kind of crap on me? How could you, Brad? What did I ever do to you?"

He was stunned by her hostility. Her eyes had taken on a deeper hurt, as if she hated him. His gut twisted when the tears popped out in her eyes. "Look, Em, I'm sorry I didn't call, I have no excuse. You've been on my mind almost every minute of the day. I just didn't know what to tell you, I've been fighting to keep my head above water with this divorce and custody of Trevor. I just didn't want you getting dragged into the middle of it."

The look she gave him at that moment, Brad wondered if she'd ever speak to him again. Then she dropped her eyes and shook her head, and stepped around him to walk away. And then changed her mind, stepped into his space, tilting her face up to his, with all the fire and fury blazing in her eyes. "Your divorce? Are you kidding me, you sure have a funny way of showing it. Have a nice holiday, Brad?" This time when she stepped back, she was walking away.

It was pure instinct to grab her arm. "Whoa, just a

second. What the hell are you talking about? What holiday?"

She rolled her eyes at him. "Don't play games, Brad. I really thought you were different; that you were someone with values and integrity. What hurts more is how you could have done that to me. You know how hard I've been struggling and it hasn't been easy finding another job."

Okay, now she really had him confused, and he felt a sticky sick feeling expand inside him like a ball being pumped with air. A few curious people milled around. They were getting loud. Brad took hold of her arm and pulled her with him to his truck parked ten feet away. He yanked open the door. "Get in now."

Chapter Thirty-Six

She couldn't believe his high handedness. What a bully. She should scream and call for help. When she glanced up, she was unprepared for his rock solid caveman routine. He was going to pick her up and toss her in. So wrenched her arm away, threw him a furious gaze, and stepped back. "No."

"Get in now or I swear I will physically put you in and really give these people an eye full. I don't know what the hell's going on, but you're going to tell me. But not here!" A few people stopped in front of the truck.

An old lady hobbled over with a cane. "Brad, dear, maybe you should let the lady go."

Emily went to step away but he slid his arm around her waist and pulled her close. "I can't do that, you see she just received some unsettling news and hasn't been acting rationally, so I need to make sure she gets home before she does or says anything that can't be undone."

"Oh, I see." The white haired lady waved as she wandered away.

Emily gaped; she wanted to yell after the woman. Tell her it was Brad who was a liar, a cheat, the devil himself. But she narrowed her eyes and climbed in, smacking his hand away when he touched her arm. The door slammed shut as soon as she cleared it.

He strode around to the driver's side, wrenched it open and climbed in. He slammed the door, gunned the engine and threw it in reverse before backing out of the parking space. He didn't say a word as he drove straight to her house, pulled up in front and turned off the engine. "Katy home?" There was no kindness in his tone.

"No." She kept her reply aloof, not willing to give anything.

He came around to her side and yanked the door open. Brad pulled her out of the truck, holding her arm and slammed the door behind her. "Let's go."

He led her up the walkway, the concrete steps and to the front door. She unlocked the door; he opened it and closed it behind them. Emily dropped her purse on the sofa and continued into the kitchen. She glanced over her shoulders. He stalked behind her like a wild animal. She needed to busy herself so she plugged in the kettle. When she turned, he was right there. So she turned around and reached for a mug in the cupboard and grabbed the box of tea. "Just leave it, Em. Turn around and look at me."

Oh good, he was as angry as she. Maybe it was better this way. Lay their cards on the table, make him look her in the eye while he explained why he had her fired. What kind of spin would he put on their holiday? She couldn't wait.

"Okay, Brad, how could you tell Jake to fire me? I still haven't found another job. I go in to apply and no one will hire me." She had to fight to control the tears, all the built up humiliation of the past few weeks. She knew she wasn't being paranoid; had he called around and asked people not to hire her? She couldn't keep her vision from blurring any more when the first tear spilled over. She couldn't see much, but she leaned back and covered her mouth when she saw his look of horror and confusion. He grabbed her arm, but this time it was filled with gentle concern, and he led her to the table.

"Sit down." A chair scraped out. Brad sat so close his legs were spread and all but surrounding hers. "What the hell are you talking about, why were you fired and when?"

"I was fired two weeks ago, right after you were here. Jake told me it was you who said to get rid of me. You even threatened to pull your account if he didn't." Her face burned when she relived that embarrassing hostile meeting. Emily jumped when his fist slammed the table, followed by explicit, quite descriptive foul curses. She'd heard him swear before, but not with this much venom.

Maybe he saw the way she pulled back, because he stopped and took her hands in his. "Em, I never told Jake to fire you. I'd never do anything like that. Not to you. Why didn't you call me?"

This time bile circled her stomach making her dizzy. She touched her forehead, and shut her eyes for a second. "Brad, I did phone. Crystal answered and I left a message for you to call me." She allowed her hand to fall into her lap. "That was when she told me you were getting ready to leave on a holiday together."

Brad leaped up. His chair hit the ground and he paced the tiny kitchen like a caged animal back and forth, clenching his fists, running his fingers through his hair. His eyes narrowed as he approached her. He watched her closely for just a minute; and then leaned closer, maybe to see if she was telling the truth.

"That bitch never gave me any message. I did not go on any holiday with her, nor would I. And I never had you fired." It was amazing how low and even, in control, his voice became when he was angry, so much so Emily feared he might hurt someone. "Why didn't you call my cell phone, Em?"

Why didn't she call his cell phone? She should've, but after she'd waited, positive she'd been played, she didn't want to talk to him. "I thought you'd played me and I didn't want to talk to you."

Brad picked up the overturned chair. He sat again, sighing as he ran his hands over his face. "Em, listen to me. I don't know what the hell's going on, but I'm starting to get a pretty good idea that Crystal's pulled some backhanded shit here. It's got her name written all over it."

He touched her head. "I'm going down to straighten out Jake. I'll be back and just so you know, I want you, Em. As soon as I get this shit with Crystal straightened out, I'm coming for you. In the meantime, don't you worry about finding another job."

She didn't know how to respond. This roller coaster ride she'd been on since she met him, she wanted it to stop. But she also worried what he'd do.

"Brad, wait. If Crystal was responsible, you need to be smart about this. Don't leave here angry. Please think about it."

He walked into her space, his arms went around her, protective and secure. His voice was gruff. "Don't worry, Em, I'll hold it together." He kissed the top of her head and smoothed back her hair with his hands.

She forced her hands up and planted them on his chest. She pushed and stepped out of his arms. "I can't do this emotional roller coaster anymore. You'll leave here; I won't see you for days—weeks. And you expect me to just sit and wait like a good little girl. I can't—won't do it anymore. No matter what Crystal did, you still hurt me. You should have called. You made love to me all night. And when I didn't hear from you, it was the same as saying it meant nothing, just another feather in your cap. I'm not made that way. I care deeply and you hurt me. So when you go out that door, to fix whatever it is you need to fix, thinking I'll be waiting for you when you're ready for me—guess again. I won't be." She wouldn't look at him. She wouldn't let him touch her as she walked around him to the sink. She gave him her back. She waited, for what she didn't know. But her heart wouldn't take anymore hurt.

Apparently he wasn't done, instead of leaving, he moved behind her. He touched her back, slid his arm around her waist. "I won't let you go. And you're right. It was my fault. I will be back. Will you still be here?"

"Go take care of what you need to." She patted his hand.

He pulled away. His heavy footsteps never broke stride as he walked out the door. And Emily never moved as she listened to his truck, the purr of the engine and spew of gravel as he drove away.

The kettle whistled, only Emily no longer needed the distraction. She pulled the plug, and sat, feeling like a woman who'd aged thirty years overnight. She was sickened by this seesaw of guilt and innocence and the awareness she'd been thrust into the middle of a playing field, with no rules to follow; winner takes all.

Chapter Thirty-Seven

Brad stormed into Jake's store; he was a man teetering on the edge of sanity.

"You get in your office now." Jake had been chatting with a customer and flushed at the heavy handedness and disrespect.

"Jackie, can you come here please. I'm sorry, George." He handled it well as he followed Brad to his office. Brad slammed the door as soon as he crossed the threshold. The short man raced behind his desk and held up his arm as if Brad would hit him.

"You fired Emily." His voice rumbled, in a quiet menacing way.

Jakes face was beet red. "You told me to fire her; you threatened to pull your account if I didn't. And you know losing your business, all the animal feed alone would hurt me. I didn't want to let her go, I liked her."

Brad slammed the side of his fist against the door. "What a load of bullshit. I never told you to fire her."

"Brad, I don't like games okay. I'm a straight shooter. But that guy who works for you, Cliff, said it was your orders. And you're the one who told me a long time ago, he speaks for you. And he said either I get rid of Emily or you were pulling all your business. So what was I supposed to do? You've always given that guy free rein."

Brad could feel the ache in his jaw as he bit down hard. It couldn't be Cliff; he trusted him. Cliff had been with him for ten years, he was like family.

"Well guess what? That was my reaction too." Jake pointed at Brad's face. "So I phoned the ranch to talk to you, because I thought for sure someone got their wires crossed. And guess what? Your wife, Crystal, answered and she was madder than a bee stuck in some old lady's bonnet. She said you were expecting him to call and confirm, and how dare I question Cliff, since he's been handling things for you for years. Plain and simple, she said you demanded she be fired. She even went so far as to say she'd tried to talk you out of it, but after all, 'you know his temper'. And once you get an idea into your head, you'd have a better chance of negotiating and reasoning with a wild animal. She said you caught her stealing money from your wallet you'd left lying in your room. She also said that you'd searched her room and discovered some of Crystal's jewelry, and the only reason you didn't press charges against her, was because of her kid. And this is your wife's quote, not mine. You refuse to do business with someone who employs a thief, a thief who stole from you."

"You know what convinced me?"

Brad leaned against the door and all that out-of-control anger changed to wariness.

"She said it would be better not to anger you any further. That just hearing Emily's name would send you over the edge. You have to admit, Brad; I've known you a lot years. I like you, but sometimes you're a hothead. And when you cut someone out of your life, you can be cruel."

That was better than an icy pail of water dumped over his head. To have someone hold up a mirror in front of you reflecting all your faults and all the stupid-ass things you've ever done.

"I'm sorry, Jake. I didn't treat you very well when I came in here. I thought you screwed Emily over, and I won't stand for someone I care about being treated that way."

Jake crossed his arms, partly relief, and the other half, righteous indignation. "Brad, you've got a temper and when you're pushed, not many of us, with any brains in our head, want to be anywhere around you."

"Jake, I don't go looking for fights. But if one comes

to my door, I'll take it on and sure as shit, I'll come out the winner."

Jake didn't move. "This isn't my fight Brad, so why's it on my doorstep?"

That was a good question.

"Crystal lied, Jake. Emily's no thief; give her back her job, today."

"I can't! I already hired Jackie. How fair is that to let her go, because of your…" He stopped his round face tinting a deep shade of pink. "Shit, Brad, what the hell's going on? You can't fuck around with people's lives like this. That was your man and your woman, which is your business. Take care of it and keep it out of mine." Jake dropped his eyes and rummaged the papers on his desk.

"Look your right, to a point, but you still should have talked to me."

He watched the man as he took on an air of indignation, snapping back at Brad in self-defense. "Well, how the hell was I to know? She's your wife."

Brad winced and brushed his hand in the air. "Jake, let's be clear on something, that's a mere technicality, soon to be rectified. And just so there are no more misunderstandings, from now on, unless you hear it directly from me, it didn't happen."

Brad yanked open the door and stalked out paying no mind to the burning eyes following him. He pressed his cell phone to his ear, stepping out of the store, he hurried to his truck. "Something's happened, got time to see me?"

"Sure, if you come right now, my next appointments in an hour."

Brad was there in ten minutes. Keith's secretary was gone for the day, so he walked right in.

Keith never looked up. "Twice in one day, what's up?"

He noticed Keith needed a haircut. His dark thick curls had grown past his ears and touched the rim of his glasses.

He filled Keith in on what happened, along with

Cliff's surprising role.

"This could be the leak, I'll call Byrd and get him to unearth everything he can on Cliff, we'll know soon enough. Since I'm sure I sound like a broken record, I'm going to remind you again to control your explosive temper. And when you speak to Cliff, because I know you, do it with some tact and use restraint. If you can manage to win him over to our side, maybe we can find out what Crystal is up to. We have a trail of where she's been for the last few years. I have to ask you, Brad. How much do you personally want to know of who she's been with?"

"You need a haircut and don't hold anything back."

Keith rolled his shoulder and tossed his pen down, chuckling under his breath. "Well okay then. She's had boyfriends, or lovers, whichever way you want to look at it; we've got names, statements. We'll use it all against her." Keith shook his head. "Glad to see it doesn't bother you. But what I'm concerned about now is this recent incident with Emily. I'm pretty sure this isn't an isolated incident. There's more. We need all we can get to show she's unfit. And let's face it, an affair when you're estranged, a judge rarely considers unless we can show the boyfriends would have been a danger to Trevor. Then it just shows poor judgment on her part and judges tend to be lenient with parents. We're not perfect."

Keith allowed Brad to mull that over for a minute. He reached for the phone and dialed.

"What are you doing?" Brad asked.

"Following a hunch, humor me." Keith winked and pressed his back into the chair, his loud voice boomed. "Hey Fred, how's the wife? How about that golf game Saturday, yah, yah, I know. Rematch?"

Brad waited and listened to the one sided conversation, not once but three times. Three local businesses; apparently the rumor mill around town had been fueled by some casual comments made by Crystal. She just happened to mention to the florist that Emily had been fired by Jake as he caught her stealing money from the till. The hardware store, Emily had tried to seduce Brad when Crystal had been downstairs looking after Trevor. She threw herself at Brad, and then vindictively searched through Crystal's jewelry and helped herself to Crystal's grandmother's emerald ring and the diamond studded earrings Brad gave Crystal for their anniversary. Apparently, Brad threw her out for her immoral behavior but was too embarrassed to press charges. The post office, which is the grapevine of the community, Crystal reported Emily was scouting for a man to support her, to move into his place, and she'd take him for everything he had. She tried with Brad, but Crystal and Brad reconciled. Emily was a scorned woman, telling stories about Crystal and Brad. And Crystal caught Emily rummaging through Brad's private papers, his business records and his bank statements, when she was supposed to be watching Trevor, who she frequently left alone. She wasn't trustworthy. She was a schemer.

Keith rested his cheek on his palm when he finally got off the phone.

"Well Emily will have a good case slander and defamation. But where to start to repair the malicious damage someone's done to your name? We'll use it in our suit against Crystal. But, Brad, you need to know something. I've been at this a lot of years. I've seen a lot of really bad people, liars, storytellers and manipulators. This type of intentional damage to someone's name, never really goes away. I just wish sometimes people would take a look at someone's motives when they're trashing a person's good name. But people live for gossip and they fuel it. Live for the drama and be dammed what it does to the poor person."

"Keith, whatever it takes, bury Crystal. Emily doesn't deserve this. And I don't want her to know."

Chapter Thirty-Eight

Two hours later, she heard his truck pull up in front of her house but she couldn't believe it. He came back.

She stood by the window, unable to move.

Brad must have seen her. He hesitated a moment and then hurried to her door. He didn't knock. He walked in and shut the door behind him.

There was no hesitation, he headed straight toward her, lifted her in his arms as if she weighed nothing more than a feather and carried her to the sofa, with her on his lap.

"What happened?" He appeared so dark and brooding; she sensed there was a whole pile of shit she didn't want to know.

"Crystal had you fired."

"Well I figured out that much myself. So what does she want with me? Why me? What did I ever do to her?" She raged the words, but she already knew. Brad. It was always about Brad.

"I'll take care of it, don't worry. I'll make sure she doesn't do this again."

Emily snapped and tried to break free. But he wouldn't let her go. "You can't make me that promise. You can no more control what she does, than control the direction the wind's blowing."

He watched her in a way she'd swear she could see the wheels spinning in his head.

"I'll make sure you're looked after and protected from anymore unprovoked attacks. I'm asking you to trust me on this." He didn't let her answer, he pulled her closer, and took what he figured was his. It was so like him to think the sun, the moon and stars revolved around him. She wanted to hit him, to hurt him, but his deep possessive kiss melted away the bitter hurt wreaking havoc on her sound reasoning. She sank into his kiss. It was a kiss that whispered silent promises of a future and the fact that she was his, and then the damn kettle shrilled. She pulled away and jumped off his lap. She needed to stop plugging it in, or maybe she should thank it, as she used those few seconds of freedom to regain her sound mind. Maybe he knew that's what she was doing, because he was right behind her, his heat, his hand covering hers when she yanked the plug from the outlet. Her blood pulsed harder, faster, through her. Her heart pounding deeper like the natives beating their sacred drums. His hand pressed flat against her back, smoothing its way down, over her shapely bottom fitted into her favorite pair of blue jeans, the ones that sat low on her hips. His hand moved over her, gently, and then changed to possessive and thorough touch. She faced the sink; he pressed into her and slid his arm around her waist. She could feel how much he wanted her. She moved her bottom against him, just as he grabbed a handful of her thick hair hanging in gentle waves down her back. He lifted it and touched his lips to the back of her neck, her shoulders, edging his way down.

His hand slid under her shirt over her stomach, her chest, outlining her curves, a little rough then tender, but he was thorough. He covered her breast, and held her against him like a man did a simple possession. Emily leaned her head back onto his shoulder, finding it difficult to breathe. She moaned as he unclasped her bra and gave her the attention she deserved. His hands moved faster as he found each tender spot, her pants loosened. How outrageously erotic as she pressed against him, and then stepped out of her pants sliding past her knees, pooling around her ankles. Her strength wavered when she felt him spread her thighs with his hand. Her breath hitched when she heard the jingle of his belt buckle, the zipper on his pants. "Brace yourself against the counter." He slipped into her, tilting her hips and holding her as if they'd mated a hundred times. Her high pitch gasp escaped. It was shockingly indecent, staring out an open window, as her man covered her hand with his, laced his fingers with hers and moved inside her as she shuddered against him, as he discovered a new spot to please her. Nothing gentle about it, pleasure met pleasure as she tightened around him. Her eyelids fluttered and she rolled her head against him; she moaned but he held on, kept going. Then he buried his face against her neck; he shouted and let himself go.

Chapter Thirty-Nine

Her legs trembled. She'd need a minute, maybe an hour before she could move again. He was still inside of her and she was momentarily shocked at how he'd taken her. If his arm wasn't wrapped around her waist, she would slide to the floor.

He nuzzled her neck, her hair. "I love the way your hair smells." He emitted a low growl in the back of his throat, and turned her around.

She didn't mind really, the smug way his lips curved, when he curled a lock of hair around his finger, before sinking down into a kiss she supposed was to be quick and light. But he sank into it.

When he pulled back an inch, and then two, his eyes were a fine slit showing the whiskey colored twinkle behind long dark lashes no man had a right to have. *God how she loved this man.* The words jammed somewhere between her heart and head. She must have stiffened, as he traced his finger across her cheek.

"Stop thinking so much, Em."

He scooped her up; her arms around his neck.

"What about your priorities, the things you need to take care of?"

"I'm tending to them now." He didn't stop; he kept going and laid her on the bed. Her mind was going fuzzy. She wrapped her arms back around his neck, and said, "What about the ranch, the animals?"

"You're first, them later."

And it was much later indeed. Brad drove Emily to the sitter's to pick up Katy. He didn't dump them and run. He stayed, he played with Katy, teased Emily and before leaving, he kissed her thoroughly and properly, the way a woman should be.

Let the games begin. Except this time, Brad had the rulebook. The sun had set when Brad parked in front of his house. He didn't move, but jingled the keys in his hand and stared at his house, his family's house, picturing the viper waiting behind the door. He understood Emily's ache, her pain. She never asked for any of this to happen. He almost lost her; he still could.

He slid out of his truck, shut the door and stopped on the bottom step. A man with a purpose, he headed toward the barn instead, where Cliff hunkered over some tack needing repairs.

"Hey, boss. Crystal was out here looking for you."

Brad put everything into each step. Maybe it was the fury on his face that had Cliff swallowing hard and backing away.

Brad bunched his fists as the fury stole over him. He wanted nothing more than to knock this young man around. Instead, he looked away, stole a breath, and then another. "Just what the hell did you think you were doing telling Jake to fire Emily?"

Cliff paled. He shifted from one foot to the other. His face lost all color. "I didn't want to do it, boss, but Crystal told me you wanted her fired. She said you asked me to stop in and give him the message. I felt bad 'cause I like Emily, but she said it was better to be done in person and you expected me to handle it for you."

"Are you kidding me? For fuck sakes, Cliff, that's the dumbest thing I think I've ever heard come out of your mouth. Try again. Because I somehow can't believe you'd think I'd relay a message like that through Crystal. And why didn't you have the fucking balls to come to me to find out what the hell was going on." Brad knew Cliff was smarter than that. His vibes poked the back of his neck. This was half-truths and he hated that bullshit.

"Before I toss your sorry ass off this ranch I want to

know something? Have you been telling Crystal what's been going on here at the ranch?" His cheeks took on a nice rosy hue. Guilty! Brad let loose a solid right jab that connected with Cliff's lip, his jaw, knocking him down.

Cliff swiped away the blood trickling from his mouth, and then touched the newly loosened tooth.

Brad reached down and grabbed Cliff's coat front, yanked him off the ground and dragged him out of the barn, giving him a hard push toward the staff house in back. "You've got twenty four hours to pack up and get off my property or I swear to God, I'll kill you with my bare hands and make damn sure your body's never found."

Brad forced himself to stay where he was as Cliff stumbled to the small white frame house he shared with Mac.

Chapter Forty

Brad fed the stock. This was Cliff's job; he'd redistribute the workload as soon as he found someone to replace Cliff.

The clouds were thick tonight; not even a sliver of moonlight seeped through. Years ago, his eyes had adjusted to the dark. He checked doors and gates, and made sure everything was fastened and secured. The front porch light illuminated two figures on the porch. As he got closer, he could see Cliff, engaged in some heated discussion with Crystal. She stopped and backed away when she saw Brad. Cliff stepped toward her, an angry man who threw up his arms in defeat and stormed away, past Brad, jumping into his beat up brown Chevy truck, spewing gravel as he drove away.

Brad really dug into each step. He slowed and then stopped on the bottom step when Crystal stumbled against the door. He took another step up. A faint flush tinted her cheeks and forehead before the icy glare appeared. "There's good old Crystal; for a moment I thought you had a conscience."

She yanked on the screen door and strode back in the house.

Brad followed the woman with not even a flicker of interest in the way she sashayed to the kitchen. He wanted to laugh, but remained quiet, calm and in control. She lifted a lid on a simmering pot on the stove, gave it a quick stir and smiled up at him. Brad knew better. Mary was here earlier and she always set dinner on the stove for Brad. He was tempted to ask Crystal what was in it. She wouldn't know. But it was vaguely entertaining to see her stumble.

"So what was that all about?" Brad couldn't wait for her spin. She was an accomplished liar and could spin a lie off the tip of her tongue as easy as she could bat an eyelash. Had she ever spoke the truth? He studied her now as he would a science experiment. What in the world made her tick?

"He told me you fired him. He wanted me to talk to you and get his job back. He told me about Emily, but I told him that I agreed with you. I mean really, how low can he get? He even threatened to tell you I told him to do it." She raised her eyes in a mock gesture of disbelief.

She was good. "Hmm." He nodded.

He couldn't help wondering now if Cliff realized she'd hung him out to dry. Tomorrow he'd make sure the detective tracked Cliff down. No maybe tonight would be better.

"Better turn that off before it burns." He said nothing more as he strode of the house.

Chapter Forty-One

The detective tracked down Cliff in the first bar he stopped at, a dingy local hangout off the highway. Cliff was sitting at the bar, pounding the counter, demanding another drink. The bartender eyed Byrd, an old NYPD cop, retired out here for the slower pace. He unzipped his tan jacket over his middle that had grown a little slack, about average for a man in his sixties.

Byrd took the stool next to him and nodded to the bartender. "Next one's on me."

"Your funeral." The big, bearded bartender with eyes that had seen everything; poured two drafts of what was on tap and slid them in front of Byrd and Cliff.

"Thanks, pal." Cliff slurred his words.

"A man sitting alone at a bar with that kind of look, reminds me of what my ex did to me, after she robbed me blind and kicked me to the curb." Byrd looked straight ahead, gazing into the mirror above the bar.

Cliff swayed as he downed a good swallow of beer. He swayed again as he leaned on the bar and stared at Byrd; a drunk looking for trouble.

"Not looking to fight with you, son. But sometimes it helps to share your troubles with a stranger." Byrd took another swallow of the cheap draft they were passing off as beer.

"What the hell would you know about be'in scammed by a pretty face, dangled for years with promises, because you're so in love with some hot babe, you'd jump through fire for her." He was really swaying now.

"Oh I think we've all been there, son, at one time in our life. Some people won't ever admit how they'd been taken advantage of as if it makes you less of a man. It don't."

Cliff guzzled the last of his beer, waved his cup in the air. "Hey, Barkeep, fill 'er up. And keep it coming." He shouted and slammed his cup on the scratched counter.

"You're done, buddy, I'll call you a cab." The bartender cut his hand in front of Byrd. "No more for your friend."

Byrd stood up and fingered out a few bills, dumping them on the counter. "I got it, I'll get him home." The bartender held up the flat of his hand and walked away.

"What, no way! I ain't drunk enough. And I plan on getting a hell of a lot drunker."

Byrd patted his shoulder, "Come on friend, I got a bottle of whiskey with your name on it."

"Yah." That got his attention. But he swayed when he stood, so Byrd helped him out to his car, and hoped to hell the kid didn't get sick.

****

He was late the next morning, but he was shorthanded with Cliff gone. Keith was speaking with an older balding guy he introduced as Byrd when he hurried in Keith's office.

"So what do you have?"

Keith extended his hand to Byrd. "Byrd, fill Brad in."

"Well your friend was pretty drunk by the time I found him. I checked him into a cheap motel by the ocean, he puked in my car by the way. You owe me for the cleaning."

"Okay." Brad shrugged. "What else?"

"That kid was twisted so tight around your wife's finger, I kind of feel sorry for him. He started working for you ten years ago, apparently him and Crystal were friends before that. She got him the job with you." Byrd had the most crooked teeth Brad had ever seen.

"I guess that's right. I think he kind of puppy dogged after her through school."

"Yah well, apparently while he worked for you, Crystal used him as her friendly ear. Whenever she needed someone to back up her side of a story, she went to him. He'd been in love with her for years, fantasizing one day she'd leave you and come looking for him. After she left, she'd call him every month or so to talk. He told Crystal when Emily moved in. He said after that, she phoned every day. And it was then she told him you threw her out, but she was too ashamed to tell him. Told him she was terrified of you and your temper, and you gave her no choice and at the time, she didn't believe she legally had any rights. She told him how worried she was about her little boy. Cliff said he had wanted to confront you. But she played the terrified, scared-helpless-female-card, and you would hurt her.

He believed her. So he searched your office when you and Emily were in town. He'd called Crystal from your office and she told him what papers to dig out. Your business records, land proposals, development permits, bank records and what kind of income you're pulling in.

But when he saw Emily in your arms one night on the porch, with your lips locked together, he phoned Crystal and told her. And that's when she came home."

****

Brad drove through town and down the highway. It was pure coincidence that had Brad pulling in the Oceanview Motel. He paid the desk clerk a hundred dollars to give up Cliff's room number. Of course, it was listed under Byrd. He pounded on the dingy blue door. "Cliff, its Brad, I need to talk to you, open up."

Glass and bottles rattled and clanked on the other side of the door. It cracked open enough for Brad to wince from the pungent raunchy odor of day old booze seeping from the pores of a drunk. Cliff slunk back to bed and held his head in his hands "You got one hell of a hangover by the looks of things."

He whispered roughly, "Look Brad, I'm done. Just go away and leave me alone."

"I want to apologize."

Cliff bolted into the bathroom. Brad closed the outside door and listened to the putrid retching and gagging as the poor guy vomited into the toilet. The odor seeped into the room when Cliff reappeared, the stale alcohol and the bitter rotgut lingering in the sweat that glazed Cliff's damp shirt and face. He shuffled like an old man to the bed. Brad cracked open a window.

"Rough night?"

"Yah." He didn't bother to look up. Just held his head as he sat slouched on the bed.

"Do you want your job back?"

He looked up and winced at the effort. "What? Now why would you give me my job back after what I did?"

"Look, Cliff. Let me ask you something and give me an honest answer. She still got you fooled?"

His bloodshot eyes narrowed. "She's conniving and she threw me to the wolves. Let me ask you this, did you throw her out after the baby?"

"Cliff, you were there. You really got to ask? She disappeared. Don't you remember the day Mary came, and she'd left Trevor alone for hours. She just took off."

He clasped his hands in front of him while he looked at Brad. His head hung. "I guess I do."

"She lied to you, didn't she?"

"Yah, she did. More than you know."

Brad didn't know what gave him more enjoyment, hearing that or watching Crystal spark in a fit of rage when she saw Cliff in his beat up truck driving in.

Cliff cleaned up before dinner and he stumbled behind Mac when he walked in. Crystal stiffened and paled. After Cliff and Mac left, Crystal cornered Brad at the back door.

"What the hell is that man doing back here?"

"I rehired him. In fact, he's now my foreman."

"After what he did, you'd bring him back. He'll steal from you; he ransacked your personal records for God's sake."

"How'd you know he went through my records?" She looked away.

She was starting to slip, too many lies to keep track of. "Well you must have told me, or maybe it was him."

"Mmm, mmm, I never told you. And Crystal, don't even think about going out to him and starting trouble. You stay away from him."

She tossed her long mane over her shoulder, flicked back a stray hair with her long painted nail and then stormed through the kitchen.

Brad tied his boots, when he heard the front door slam and her SUV speed down the driveway. Brad laughed. "Scored."

Chapter Forty-Two

Brad was on his second cup of coffee when the phone rang. "Brad here."

"Hey, it's Keith. We got us a court date for next Tuesday. The judge has finally agreed to expedite for the benefit of Trevor. Oh, and I got a really friendly call as soon as I walked in the office this morning from Crystal's lawyer. He's furious and has filed a motion to delay this hearing."

"Can he get it?" Brad stepped out of the house to make sure Crystal couldn't hear him.

"I'll do my best to make sure he doesn't. And I wanted to let you know, I've got several affidavits about Crystal and the defaming comments she's made around town against Emily. Along with Cliff's statement, and thank you for that, her story is beginning to appear shaky."

"Well, you're the best. That's why I hired you." He could hear tapping in the background.

"Brad, could you come to the office right now." Keith's tone took on a seriousness Brad recognized well.

"What's going on, Keith? I've got cattle to feed, a ranch to run." But his stomach tightened a little more when he heard the sigh on the other end.

"Get your men to look after the ranch. You need to come in. This can't wait."

Brad stared up at the house as he walked around in the chilly air to the front. "I'll be there in twenty minutes."

* * * *

Brad was waved into Keith's office. The secretary

pulled the door closed behind him. Keith smiled but not in a confident way. It was his way when he had to say something to someone he didn't want to.

"Spill it, Keith, you're making me nervous with all this prancing around."

"Crystal's lawyer has thrown a monkey wrench into the middle of things."

Brad leaned back in the plain brown chair. "And what would that be?"

Keith leaned forward and clasped his hands on the desk in front of him. His eyes dimmed. "Crystal's claiming Trevor's not yours. The father is some guy she met in Miami." The room narrowed and Keith appeared to be talking in slow motion. The ringing in his ears buzzed long and loud as the ache in his heart swelled until he'd swear, it'd shatter into a million tiny pieces. He launched himself out of the chair "I'll kill her. I swear to God, she's dead!" Keith jumped out of his chair and pinned him against the wall.

"Shut up, Brad. Listen to me." If Keith hadn't kept himself in such good shape, there'd be no way he'd be able to keep Brad in that room. Even so, Keith was sweating as he forced Brad back in his chair.

"Brad, get a hold of yourself." He stood over Brad, breathing hard as he held his arms loosely at his side, obviously prepared to grab Brad if he bolted again.

"We'll order a paternity test today. Brad, I got to warn you, if it turns out he's not yours, it'll make the custody battle a little tougher. Not impossible, don't forget on the birth certificate, she named you as the father. You still want him if he's not yours?"

Brad shoved Keith as he jumped out of the chair. "God dammit, he's my boy. I don't care what comes back, that's my little boy. Do you hear me?" The pain consuming him thickened his words.

Keith reached out and squeezed his shoulder. "Hey, I'm on your side. I'll make the arrangements to confirm paternity, but heed me well, Brad. Until this is over, move out. Unless you can guarantee you can cool that temper of yours and not do anything stupid; you stay away from her. Pack your bags and move out. Move to one of those cottages on your property. And you make sure you're never alone with her. I don't care how, but you find a way. We're too close, this is the final battle, my friend. Don't blow it."

Brad listened but he wanted her gone, whatever it took. Crystal knew exactly what buttons to push. The more Keith talked the less he heard. "I can't stay here. I need to clear my head."

"You promise me, Brad, before you walk out that door, that you'll pull it together and not do anything stupid."

He knew what Keith was saying and he didn't know if he could do it. "I'll try Keith, that's all you're going to get." Then he left feeling numb.

He didn't know how long he sat in his truck, or how he got here. But he climbed out of the truck and she was there, her hands in the dirt with Katy beside her.

Chapter Forty-Three

Emily froze just looking at the sadness that hunched him over when he leaned against the truck. Emily went to him. She took his hand. She led him to the house. "Katy, time to come in the house."

She let go of Brad's hand and watched as he walked, like a man who'd lost everything, into the kitchen and stood before the sink, staring out her small square window.

Emily popped in a movie for Katy, tucking her blanket around her on the sofa. She grabbed the phone.

"Hey sugar, what's cooking." She answered on the first ring.

"Gina, something's happened. I need a big favor. Can you come and get Katy?"

"Can you talk about it?"

"Not now, Gina. I realize this is short notice … and I promise I'll tell you later."

"I'll be right there."

Emily hung up the telephone. She came up behind Brad and slipped her arm around his waist. "Gina's coming to get Katy. Brad, you're scaring me. What's happened?"

He turned around and stared down at her with a face that resembled granite. He didn't touch her. His arms hung at his side, as he gazed down, his eyes glistened with tears. He touched her face, right before his jaw trembled.

She wiped away the tear that fell just as a car pulled up. "Gina's here. I'm going to throw some stuff in a bag for Katy so she can spend the night, I'll be right back."

Emily had a quick chat with Gina, packed Katy's bag and had her out the door in less than five minutes. When she walked back into the kitchen, Brad had put on a pot of coffee. His jacket tossed over the back of her cheap wooden chair. He'd regained his dignity.

She took his hand and pulled him into the living room, sitting beside him on the sofa. "What's happened?"

He looked away for just a moment. "Crystal said Trevor's not my kid."

Emily felt the fire burn inside, and for the first time ever, she considered and understood how a spouse could kill another.

"Emily, I haven't told Keith this, but Crystal went away several times that year, before she knew she was pregnant. Shopping trips she called them."

Emily was furious and couldn't contain the words that spewed forth, "Oh, that bitch. Oh, Brad how could she do that to you and that precious little boy?"

Brad pulled her against him. Wrapped his arms around her and comforted her. "Do you know how beautiful you are to me, especially when you're angry?"

He kissed the top of her head, as she rested her cheek against his dark blue shirt. "What are we going to do?"

Just the fact that she automatically assumed it was the two of them in this made the pain lessen a little.

They talked for hours trying to come up with a viable plan of attack. It was after nine o'clock and neither had eaten. He pulled away from her and stood up. "I have to go, Em."

"Brad, please stay."

"I can't, not tonight. I got to get my head together and I can't do it here."

Her face must have portrayed her hurt.

"Em, don't look like that. You're my rock and I feel things for you I've never felt for any woman, not this deep. But I have to take care of something."

She was reluctant to let him leave. "Em, I promise I'll come back tomorrow morning." He touched her cheek and she leaned into his hand. Then he left, before she managed to talk him into staying. From his darkened truck he watched her. She pressed her hand to the glass as he pulled away.

Chapter Forty-Four

He called his daddy from the truck. He answered on the first ring, of course he sounded groggy because they were asleep. He explained Crystal's latest stunt, and arranged for the paternity test. His father offered up all his resources and his lawyers to ensure this came out in Brad's favor. In the end, Brad agreed and gave his daddy permission to go ahead and contact Keith, to extend all pertinent resources to him.

He kept his word with Emily. After he fed the stock in the morning, got the men organized; he stopped in to see her. Maybe to reassure her he wasn't about to do anything stupid.

Over the next few days, Brad did his best to avoid Crystal. Although she made it difficult, placing herself directly in his path at every opportunity. She goaded him. And on the second day, after the paternity test was in, she followed him to town, and tried to corner him outside his lawyer's office.

"Get out of my way."

"I want to talk to you, please, Brad." He struggled to suppress his fiery temper and walked around her.

He walked right into Keith's office and sat down.

"She followed me to town, cornered me out front."

Keith got up and looked out the window. "That woman's got balls or is just plain stupid. Don't see her; she must have gone."

"So what's the news?"

Keith tossed him the envelope with the results. Brad reached out and held the envelope. For the first time in his life, he wanted to run; not face it. How could one piece of paper have the power to change his life forever? He closed his eyes. His throat tightened and he felt tentacles squeeze his heart. He forced himself to rip it open; pull out the sheet of white paper. He opened his eyes and gazed at the results and couldn't hold back the sting of tears. His lip trembled as he looked up at his longtime friend, who for the first time since this started, had tears in his eyes. Brad shut his eyes, and wept.

Chapter Forty-Five

Brad waited in the kitchen until he was ready. Then he strode to the stairs and shouted, "Crystal, get down here." He watched as she started down the stairs. Her heels clicked on each step. He wandered back in the kitchen and leaned against the stove. When she stepped into the kitchen, he stood like a general leading his troops.

"Sit down, now." His voice was quite controlled considering the circumstances.

She appeared to consider her options as she glanced at the door, and then him.

Then with a toss of her long blonde hair and a subtle sway in her hips, she walked over to the chair pulled away from the table and sat down.

Brad felt ill for the wasted years of chasing her. He stepped behind her and she squirmed in the chair, crossing and uncrossing her legs. She started to get up, "Sit your ass back in that chair." He walked in front of her and leaned in her face as he said it.

He pointed to the envelope in front of her on the table. "That's for you and it's my final offer. You either sign it now and get the fuck out of my house, or you get nothing." He wandered over to the counter.

She gazed at the tan manila envelope.

"Open it." His words were void of any emotion, steely and hard, which caused a shadow of fear and confusion to flicker across her face. Her hand trembled when she picked it up and slit it open with a carefully manicured nail.

He watched as she read it; watched the range of emotions that flickered across her face, and finally as she tossed the papers aside shaking her head with a spark of fury registering in her cold blue eyes. "I'm not signing this and there is no way Trevor—"

He cut her off as he uncrossed his arms, gripping the side of the counter in an attempt to steady himself from his rising temper. "Don't you say one word about Trevor."

Her mouth snapped shut and the first time ever, he saw fear on her face.

"My lawyer's preparing, right now at this moment, to file a motion, terminating all your rights as a parent. Of course, it's a crapshoot, but a very real possibility, especially after the stunt you just pulled.

Included in this motion will be not one single dime for you and that, my dear, is a very real possibility. You see, after your wonderful little bit of acting, imagine our surprise to once again see you spin another web of your lies. The paternity test came back. You'll be happy to note, Trevor's mine. But then, you already knew that didn't you?" He didn't allow her to answer. Instead he walked toward her clasping his hands behind his back as he steadied himself. He then began pacing back and forth as her face paled. "So you have two choices. You either pick up the pen and sign the agreement right now, giving me sole custody and guardianship of Trevor, and do not contest the divorce decree, which is before a judge as we speak, and then you may keep the very generous settlement I'm offering. As you can see in black and white in front of you, it's a lot of money. And then I want you to leave and never show your face here again, ever. If you choose to fight this, get up and walk away without signing it. I'll have an injunction to have you removed from the premises right now and you will not get a dime. I've already cut you off financially. And any bills I get on your behalf, will be returned unpaid. I'm no longer responsible for you. You'll have to get a job and support yourself. Especially once the judge sees all the evidence against you. The abandonment of Trevor, when you left him alone, the slander against Emily, which we have statements for and very willing people to testify against you, but the last bit, lying about Trevor's paternity, tsk, tsk." He shook his head feeling steady control as he watched her hesitate, before biting the side of her lip.

"As for Trevor, don't add harming an innocent child to your list of follies." For the first time ever, she actually flushed in embarrassment. "You should also know, Emily has a very good case against you for slander and defamation of character. Did you know the courts are now handing out some very large settlements? Her hands were in her lap, but he knew she was shaking inside. "Sign it, Crystal. Walk away today. As you can see, I'm being extremely generous. There'll be no suit from Emily and no action will be brought against you, but only if you sign. I'm sure your lawyer will be able to advise you of your chances of winning a slander and defamation suit of this degree. Your choice. Right now. You don't want me for an enemy. Even you can't be that foolish." He noted her hesitation, the uncertainty.

She picked up the pen that had been placed precisely beside the envelope. Her hand shook as she turned to the tabs clearly marking where she needed to sign. After signing and initialing each page, she threw down the pen and rose from the chair.

"Pack your bags and get the hell out of my house now. The money will be in your account as soon as this is filed." Without a word, she hurried upstairs.

Chapter Forty-Six

Brad sat out on the front porch breathing in the cool night air on this unusually warm spring night, smiling at the way things had turned out. The day he received the news in Keith's office flooded him with sweet, overwhelming relief. To have Crystal gone and out of their lives was a black tension-filled cloud dissipated. Even the sunshine seemed to beam brighter around them. Crystal had left town right after signing the papers, leaving instructions for the rest of her belongings to be sent to a condo in Seattle.

Keith filed the papers that day. He pulled strings to have a judge sign the divorce decree a few days later. Thirty-one days and he'd be a free man.

For the first time in his life, he felt as if he was living life with his eyes wide open. "You know, Dad, I'm glad you and Mom are going to stay for a bit."

Brad's father clinked his glass to Brad's. "Here's to a good woman, your son and finally getting it right." He swallowed the single malt scotch, and turned when the screen door squeaked.

"Are the kids asleep?"

Emily rested her hand on his shoulder.

When he looked up into the passion burning in her sparkling eyes, a lump formed deep in his throat. She took his breath away.

"I'll leave you two lovebirds alone." Rodney stopped and rested his hand fondly on Emily's shoulder, looking down on her as a father would his daughter.

"Thanks, Dad." Brad reached around and lifted Emily onto his lap.

"Mmm, yep, all fast asleep."

He leaned his head down and kissed the tip of her nose. She still couldn't believe he'd done it. Showing up, ordering his men to pack up all their things and move them back out to the ranch. He hesitated for only a moment, and informed her he loved her. And as soon as both their divorces were final, he planned to marry her.

The way he looked down on her with such everlasting desire, friendship and love; she knew he'd just handed her his heart. For him, it was a rare gift of trust.

Sitting on his lap now, his fingers linked with hers, she knew they had a future filled with possibility.

"You never answered me, Em."

She slid around on his lap and wrapped her arms around his neck. "Answer you about what?"

"I think I asked you to marry me. And you've left me hanging."

She caressed his face with the back of her fingers, unable to remember her heart ever being so full. "If I recall, you informed me we were getting married. But the answer's yes."

She snuggled a little closer, she couldn't wait to share the news with him. She took his hand and placed it on her stomach as a slight blush rose in her cheeks. The doctor said the baby would be born in November.

About the Author

Lorhainne Eckhart began her writing career in 2008, when she published her first novel, The Captain's Lady, a Contemporary Military Romance through The Wild Rose Press. You can find Lorhainne most days on Twitter, Facebook, Goodreads, contributing posts to her two blogs The Choice of Giving and Illusions while actively promoting her books, The Forgotten Child, The Captain's Lady, her supernatural romantic suspense series, The Choice, and a children's illustrated adventure, A Father's Love.

Lorhainne Eckhart is a member of the RWA, Sisters in Crime and Victoria RWA. She writes edgy romantic suspense and warns her readers to expect the unexpected. The mother of three children, one a special needs child. They live on a small back water Island in the Northern Gulf where Lorhainne advocates for the environment, and rights of special needs children. And somewhere in her busy schedule she finds time to write. Readers can contact her through her Website
www.LorhainneEckhart.com

Or Email: Lorhainne@LorhainneEckhart.com

Her latest novel, The Forgotten Child, is a contemporary romance. And explores the devastating issue of Autism Spectrum Disorder. For more information about autism contact your local Autism Society and:
FEAT (Families for Early Autism Treatment)
Autism Speaks

Made in the USA
Lexington, KY
21 February 2013